Princess Mimi's Magical Quest

By

Julia Robinson

Library of Congress Control Number: 2024900163

Copyright © 2023 by Julia Robinson

All rights reserved. No portion of this book may be reproduced in any form without written permission from the publisher or author except as permitted by U.S. copyright law.

Dedication

This book is dedicated to my older sister, Elinor Jane Ingram. She spent 42 years teaching in rural Wyoming communities. She assisted me in the development of the plot and in ensuring that the narrative was appropriate and interesting to middle-grade readers.

Acknowledgment

A big shout out to The Native Publishers, San Francisco, California, and Xavier Blythe, the Account Manager, and his team specifically James Peterson, The Head of Content, for transforming my rough draft into a publishable product.

TABLE OF CONTENTS

Prologue 1

Chapter 1: Paradise Lost 4

Chapter 2: Maribel and the Remaining Saphire Clan 12

Chapter 3: Homeless 16

Chapter 4: The Enchanted Burl 23

Chapter 5: A Time to Heal 31

Chapter 6: Evacuate 38

Chapter 7: Gypsy Fortune Teller 43

Chapter 8: The Elfin Way 50

Chapter 9: Mimi Finds Her Way 57

Chapter 10: Encounter with the Goblins 68

Chapter 11: Wizard Island 73

Chapter 12: Battle with the Goblins 80

Chapter 13: Welcome by a Gnome 87

Chapter 14: Professor Magnus and the Magic Book 96

PROLOGUE

Mimi squirmed in the hard gold chair next to the big throne.

Her sister Maribel floated slowly down the red carpet. Maribel's name meant beauty. She looked gorgeous as always. She was wearing the Sapphire's clan traditional outfit. A long blue velvet skirt with a blue-white tartan scarf tied over her white silk blouse. The royal blue color exactly matched her skin. Her long straight white hair shined silver in the sun.

Mimi had always been envious of her older sister's appearance, especially her big cobalt wings. They glowed iridescent in the sunlight. Colorful patterns bounced off them reflecting an array of designs in blue shades on the tree house walls. When Maribel's wings were in full furl in the big hall at mid-day the glow from the sun was impressive. Mimi liked to stare around the hall at all the colors and shapes. She imagined she was looking through a kaleidoscope, all the patterns swirling around her.

When Maribel got to the front of the great hall, she smiled at Mimi. Her stunning violet eyes crinkled at the corners. She turned around to the crowd with a swish of her wings. All the Sapphire fairies in the room shouted her name, "Maribel, Maribel!" Maribel acknowledged them by waving and smiling.

Maribel was becoming the leader of her clan. Mimi wanted to be happy for her. She still missed her mother and father. Just two days ago, both of her parents had been crushed by a drone that flew too close. All that was left were broken wings and the clan's medallion pieces.

The shouting stopped. The Sapphire Wizard brought out the magic medallion on a blue velvet pillow. The medallion was gold on a long chain. On the medallion was a gorgeous fig tree with a giant leaf canopy and long roots. The leaves were covered with sparkling blue fairy lights. The base of the tree was surrounded by jade. The design looked just like their home, Cyan Castle.

The Wizard lifted half of the medallion and the color went out of it. Maribel, who was quite tall for a fairy, bent down. The Wizard placed the chain and medallion over her head.

"Mimi come forward," the Wizard said. Mimi looked around.

She didn't like attention. At 13, she was short, only 6 inches compared to her sister's glorious 10-inch height. She was a little pudgy. Her mom had blamed her shape on "baby fat." But her friends sometimes called her "chubby." Worst of all her skin and hair were pale pastel blue, the color of mold on rotting cheese. She still had baby wings. She should have sprouted her permanent wings when she turned 12.

Her mom said, "she was a slow bloomer." Her little wings embarrassed her. She couldn't fly as fast as her friends. They were always practicing with their new brightly colored big wings. Sometimes they would flap them at her just to blow her off course.

She'd struggle to right herself. They'd laugh and tease, "Mimi, mini wings. She's got fins, like her fishy friends."

Her mom told her, "Your friends are bullying you. They shouldn't do that."

One-time Maribel flew by just as Mimi's attackers were singing the hated fish song. Maribel shot out of the sky on her big wings like a hawk. She hovered backwards, smacked her wings together hard, and blew the fairy tweens across the sky. One did a somersault. Another hit a tree. Maribel whirled around hoovering. She drew her wand, no longer twisted because she was 18. She shook it at them. Sparkly starbursts shot out the end, like a twinkler on the 4th of July.

"You do that again to my kid sister and you'll have to deal with my wand." The bullies looked terrified.

"As they should," thought Mimi. Maribel was a strong woman, not to be messed with.

Mimi felt like she'd been walking for an hour with everyone staring at her. But she'd only taken three or four steps. Unlike Maribel, the Wizard towered over her.

"Mimi, do you promise to be the second in command? To help your sister, Maribel lead the Sapphires. When there is danger, do you promise to take care of everyone who lives in Cyan Castle?" Mimi would do anything for Maribel. She just wasn't sure what it could be because she didn't have the skills Maribel possessed in flying, strength, magic, looks, anything.

Mimi nodded her head up and down and whispered, "Yes!"

The Wizard placed the other half medallion over Mimi's head. The chain hung down to her waist. "You must keep the medallion safe. When the medallion pieces are combined, the power of the clan is doubled. In times of peace and plenty, we don't need that much power. We don't want anyone to misuse it. We must make sure that only a Sapphire has both pieces. Mimi, do you promise to protect the medallion at all times?" the Wizard asked.

"Yes," Mimi promised solemnly.

The clan broke into shouting and dancing. The next generation of Sapphire clan leaders, the sisters Maribel and Mimi LaFae, had been installed.

CHAPTER 1: PARADISE LOST

The day had started out like any other warm spring day. Well, if Mimi was honest, better than most days. When she got up, she'd thrown open the wooden shutters blocking light into the tree house. Sun had streamed in along with music from the human campers' boom box, "Shake it off" by Taylor Swift, one of Mimi's favorite songs. The sun and the song were both good omens.

Mimi grabbed her twisted wand and started dancing, right-left, wand in the air one-two. As she danced around her room, she used her wand to pick up the party dresses she'd tossed all over the floor last night. "Leotard, off the floor, hang on the hook to the right. Lacy dress swing on a hanger out of sight."

The music ended. She could hear the campers packing up in a hurry saying something like "needing to move fast."

She slipped on her dress for the Fairy Tea Festival. She'd tried on a bunch of outfits, accounting for the floor mess but had decided on her favorite sun dress with a Bluebird feather skirt sewn on a stretchy top covered with shiny silver trinkets collected by her bird friends. She wanted to look her best. As second in command of the Sapphires, some of the mean faes were treating her nicer. She was looking forward to a good time at the tea. Maybe even making a friend.

As she poked, a peacock feather into her hair, Mimi heard, "Tattahat-at." An erratic flutter of many wings. Something was wrong.

Her stomach lurched. Chills flickered up her slim blue neck. Diminished flight is one of a fairy's greatest fears. Mimi's wings fluttered rapidly with her increasing heartbeat. She lifted a couple of inches off the tree house floor. A bead of sweat rolled down her smooth glacier-blue forehead. The saltiness stung one sparkling aquamarine eye. Tears started running down her chin.

"Be brave!" she scolded herself. "You're a fearless fairy leader, not a silly chipmunk."

The fairy scouts had been on a food-gathering quest. The constant whir of many wings flapping was their routine sound when returning to the castle. This buzz was irregular. "Rattat-ta-tat-Buzz whirr, ratata-whirr." Off-beat, discordant, upsetting.

The wings' staccato beating was now accompanied by the "E-YE-E" of a Peregrine Falcon, sounding the alarm. The great bird's voice echoed through the sky. The soprano wrens started tweeting. The robins' deep-throated tenor echoed back. "Chirp, cheep, chirp." The crows and ravens were now cawing loudly directly overhead. A fearsome racket indeed! The feather flock warning brigade was in full voice. Mimi spoke bird. But a translation wasn't necessary. Something was terribly wrong. As the whirring got closer, Mimi could smell smoke off in the distance.

"Fire! Evacuation!"

She knew everyone would have to leave. Mimi grabbed her royal blue backpack hanging by the door. She picked it for the color. The size and shape weren't very handy for carrying equipment. The darker blue had looked amazing against her pale blue complexion. She didn't care about how it worked. She was sometimes messy tossing her wispy fairy gowns around her room. She always put her backpack and twisted wand away by the door. She might be called out at any moment to assist her fellow fairy clan members.

She quickly peaked in her pack. Yep, her wand was glowing, a light blue, fully charged, radiating from inside the bag. She pulled her family medallion off her neck and dropped it in the pack. She didn't want the heavy gold and jeweled piece to hold her back. She was going to need all her energy to help others escape.

She swung the pack up on her back wishing she had time to put on her flight suit. Instead, she flew towards the tree hole in her bulky morning glory, blue feather gown. The billowing skirt and puffed sleeves held her back. She had just pinned peacock feathers in her long blue hair to go out for the tea party with girlfriends. She'd been taught in emergencies to move swiftly and leave everything behind.

When she got to the door, she pulled the emergency lever on the wall. A high-pitched who-oo, who-oo shrieked through the air. The ongoing rumble through the fig tree and its root system told the Sapphire clan to evacuate.

The entire fig tree started shaking. Mimi could hear the sharp popping of hardened figs falling on the ground, combined with the angry chattering of the squirrels who lived above, in the canopy.

There were a couple of fairy "Owies!" and "That hurt!" as the dropping figs hit escaping fairies.

"There," she thought, "If the bird call didn't get everyone moving the fairy emergency warning system would."

As she peeked out through the knot hole, she could see flames jumping high. The sky was red. Fire galloping across the western skyline. Gray smoke clouds were rolling towards her. In front of the clouds, dust billowed kicked up by a menagerie of fleeing animals. There was a mountain lion in the lead followed by two bobcats, a herd of deer, and many small critters all running for their lives. The sky was entirely gray, full of flying birds and smoke.

Closer to her, but substantially diminished in number were the fairy scouts. They were flying in a disorganized pattern, totally uncharacteristic of them. The scouts had gone out at dawn on their regular food-gathering patrol. She could see Maribel rapidly spinning, a high-speed deflector, sending out fast wind with her wings. She was directing the other scouts around the grove towards the river.

Maribel looked towards the fig tree. She shot an air dart from her wand at Mimi. A direct hit with hot air. "Bam!", like a hot slap on the back of her head. Mimi was gobsmacked. How could her sister be so mind-blowingly accurate? From such a distance too! Then she realized Maribel was warning her to get moving.

Mimi had never been in a major fire but had read about them in books. The soot from fires can coat fairy wings causing a fairy to drop like a dead weight. Mimi's cousin had accidentally burned a wing while curling her hair with a hot curling iron. Her "yelp" of pain told Mimi to be careful when fixing her own long blue locks. But more horrifying to Mimi than the pain was the way her cousin's wounded wing slowly curled inside like melted wax, interfering with her ability to fly and taking weeks to heal.

"Oh, dear," she thought. "We've lost a lot of scouts. Maribel's right to head towards the water. I'll get everyone in the grove going to the river too."

She joined the other fliers: her fairy neighbors, dragonflies, butterflies, and birds as they all headed towards the river and hopefully safety. She was flying as fast as she could. Her baby wings were pulsating rapidly up and down like a hummingbird. She was panting. Mimi's tears had transformed into rivers of sweat, running down her face and pitting her arms. "Oh, how I wish I had permanent wings."

Red Robin swooped in blocking Mimi's trajectory and chirping hysterically.

Mimi asked, "Do you need help?"

Red Robin headed towards her nest where Mimi saw three little fuzzy heads with open beaks peaking over the top.

"Oh no!" she thought. "Red won't leave her babies behind."

Mimi called out, "Red, coming! I'll help you."

She flew over to a long vine trailing down a tree. She pulled out her twisted wand from the backpack, "TING!" She clipped off a long vine. She flew towards the nest dragging the vine behind her. Red was circling frantically. Mimi ran one end of the vine through the nest and pushed it between the baby robins and out the other side.

She called Red, "Come! Grab both ends and lift." She held the ends of the vine out for Red to clutch in her beak.

Red Robin dove down and grabbed the ends of the vine. She slowly pulled up. Mimi held her breath hoping the nest would hold together as it was dislodged from the tree. Little twigs, pieces of cotton, and other nest materials floated by Mimi. But the nest held as Red pulled up. The robin started flying slowly towards the river with her precious cargo swinging below. The nest and babies reminded Mimi of an upside-down parachute. She looked around and saw other fairies helping birds save their babies. Soon the sky was full of nests moving slowing towards the river with their precious baby bird cargo.

Mimi hovered in place to look back and saw the fire gaining on the fleeing animals. Flames were gobbling up everything, trees, slower animals, the entire forest. Below her, animals were scurrying away from the smoke. Birds up high were circling looking for safe places as the fire jumped back and forth blocking pathways keeping them from moving forward.

The Peregrine falcon, the fastest of the group, had gone out to the river and come back several times. Flying high in the sky, wings wide, shouting, "E-E-y-E." The falcon's call signaled the right direction for those on the ground and traveling in smokey air.

Over on the human road, she saw a traffic jam. Cars trying to flee were backed up and not moving. There was only one road out of Paradise. The fire would soon catch the cars.

People started abandoning their cars and running, joining the fleeing animals. The running people added further chaos to the fire, screaming, shouting, falling down, and jumping up. Some of them stepped on or stumbled over animals in their path.

Mimi made a hard right to avoid the humans. A gust of wind whipped ash all over her.

The heavy gray particles acted like a suit of armor dragging her down. She was flapping her wings as hard as she could, but she was no longer moving forward. She was barely maintaining in one place. She worked harder, flapping with all her might, constantly sweating, and panting. She hurriedly looked back again. The fire was closing in. Her wings were starting to melt. She was about to be singed by the raging flames.

She started coughing. She was dropping as the smoke entered her lungs and slowed her ability to fly. The tips of her wings were folding inward from the heat making flying almost impossible. She started feeling a sharp pain on the farthest part of her wings nearest the fire. She couldn't see. She was sucking in smoke. She felt very peaceful like she was floating. Her mom was beckoning her. She felt very confused. Her mom and dad were dead. Where was she?

Just as she was about to give into the hazy dream world and drift downward, she heard the call of the Peregrine falcon EEEE-y-EE close to her ear. The bird was dive bombing. Faster and faster he came at her, eyeing her like prey. The swish of his wings blew fresh air at her. She shook herself out of her fantasy and breathed cool, clean $H2O$.

Seeing the falcon coming even closer, she curled into a ball, terrified. His giant talons could shred her skin. When he reached her, he grabbed her backpack. He yanked her from the clutches of the cloying gray smoke and shot straight up out of the muck. Traveling at over 200 miles an hour, Mimi felt she was attached to a rocket. She shut her eyes tight to avoid the pain of the rapid air. Tears were pouring down her face. Her wings were tattered. Little shards broke away with the falcon's propulsion. Feathers and trinkets from her dress tore off. Her long blue hair was yanked straight back by the air velocity as the falcon shot through the sky away from the noise, the smoke, the fire to the clear air.

Mimi was exhausted but slowly she felt fresh air coming into her lungs. She could breathe again. Once above the smoke, the falcon leveled off and started to soar, opening his blue-grey wings wide.

The force of the bird's strong propulsion was no longer making her eyes water.

Mimi opened her eyes. She stared down below her. There was total chaos. Smoke and flames were catching up with the slowest. The fire was indiscriminate in its destruction. She saw humans stumble and animals disappear into the flames. Some birds carrying nests were getting near the river. Others were disappearing into the smoke. She spotted Red Robin.

"Almost there, Red," she thought. "Fly faster." The falcon soared over the river. Safety zone.

He swooped down and dropped Mimi, plunk on the outstretched limb of a giant redwood. She landed unceremoniously on her butt. A tree needle stuck her in the arm causing trickles of blue blood to seep from the small holes in her skin. Another needle was tangled in her hair. She inhaled the pungent forest smell, a reminder that she was safe from the smoke.

She felt like a poster on a bulletin board, stuck up with pins. She started untangling herself as the falcon flew away, leaving her behind on her sticky perch.

She could see she was across the river, but very high in the tree. The entire valley was on fire. The flames were spreading everywhere, a red flame army, marching forward leaving black scarred trees and desolate land and burned skeletons behind.

She had never been this high in a tree before. Her tree hollow in the fig tree had been her home for as long as she could remember. Her home was below the branches, safe from the squirrels who guarded the green leafy canopy above. Now she was near the top of a giant tree with no leaves only needles. She couldn't see any of her friends or Maribel from her perch. She was injured and couldn't fly. She was thirsty and hungry. She was safe from the fire but homeless and alone in a new country.

CHAPTER 2: MARIBEL AND THE REMAINING SAPHIRE CLAN

Maribel was spinning extremely fast. Her dark blue coloring transformed to white, like a spinning color wheel matching her hair. She used the air current generated by the snapping propulsion of her big wings Woosh! Woosh! Each rotation pushed the other members of the fairy brigade forward. Away from the blazing forest fire towards the safety of the river.

She looked through the aspens and spied the knot hole she called home. Was that a bluebird sitting at the entrance? How odd! Surely that wasn't Mimi, her little sister, popping her head out, covered with blue feathers. Why wasn't she in her flying suit? She should be getting everyone at Cyan Castle out of harm's way.

Maribel loved Mimi but sometimes she was just too weird. Well, now was not the time to hesitate. Maribel lifted her wand arm, aimed straight at those stupid feathers. "Air fly like a dart, make Mimi smart." She didn't even wait to see if the dart hit Mimi, she knew her aim was true and straight. She hoped the smack would knock those stupid feathers off Mimi's head. A fire was not the time to be dressed to go out to a party.

She must have been going out with those silly mean fairies.

Maribel couldn't understand why Mimi didn't make new friends. She'd had to break up a bullying session just the other day. Why would anyone spend time with fae who were mean to you? Her sister was a quandary to her. She didn't know what to do. With their parents recently killed, and the clan to protect, she didn't have a lot of time left for a 13-year-old and her many problems.

She pushed the last of the brigade past her towards the river. Lots of scouts lost but many had been saved by the swirling air from her big wings. Now she needed those wings to get her to the river to help everyone once they were there.

With the last of the scouts sailing towards the river, Maribel unfurled her wings and snapped past her brigade. By the time they reached the river, most of the flyers from the Aspen Grove and fairies from Cyan Castle were already wading into the water or buzzing back and forth along the shoreline.

Maribel started looking for Mimi. She knew she'd given her adequate warning with the dart to the head to get moving. She asked numerous creatures if they had seen Mimi. For those who didn't know her, Maribel pointed to her medallion and asked for a pale blue fairy wearing a similar decoration. Maribel didn't know Mimi hadn't been wearing the memorable piece but had tossed it in her backpack.

Maribel finally talked to Red Robin who described how bravely Mimi had helped her save her children. The last time Red saw Mimi, she was struggling, coughing, and inhaling smoke. Red had flown back after getting her nest to safety on the other side of the river. But she couldn't find Mimi in the billowing smoke clouds. Red told Maribel, "Mimi might be lost."

Maribel collapsed to her knees sobbing. She was always so critical of Mimi. She should have handled the exit of Cyan Castle herself. She blamed herself for leaving the task to Mimi. She had seen it as a simple job of ringing the warning bell. But she had not thought of kindhearted Mimi making every effort to not only get the fairy clan out safely but also the other fliers. Almost everyone from the castle birds, squirrels, and fairies were accounted for. Mimi had completed her task well.

As Maribel was quietly crying for her sister, one of her guards tapped her on the shoulder. The fire was nearing the river. Soon there would be no ground left. While most of the fairies could fly, some were injured. Maribel stood up and took on the cloak of being a leader. She started directing the fliers to move downstream and find a place without smoke and flames.

For those who could not fly, she started working with the brigade to identify vessels, sticks, large leaves, or anything that could float down the river. Within minutes everyone was moving south, down the river away from the vast smoke and flaming trees.

Maribel helped the last wounded fairy onto a small log along with several other burned fliers. She used her long straight wand to push the vessel into the river. "Magic wand give a push, make this log go like a ship."

Rushing air came roaring out of the wand. The log pushed forward catching the river current. The makeshift boat floated rapidly downstream. The fairies on board were shrieking. She didn't know if it was from joy or fear or like a rollercoaster a combination of both.

Behind her, she heard the eye-o-e of the Peregrine falcon. She turned to wave. Glad to know the great bird had survived the fire. He landed next to her. Maribel like Mimi spoke bird. As soon as he landed he started talking, "I grabbed your little sister from the flames."

Maribel was thrilled. "Where is she?"

"Things were bad," the great bird said, "She wasn't flying, and I couldn't see. I got her out of the fire and dumped her in a redwood tree up stream."

"Oh, show me where and I'll go get her."

"That's the problem. You haven't seen me because I already went to get her. She wasn't there. I checked all the trees. She's gone."

Maribel's eyes got big, "You lost her in the forest. She wasn't doing well!"

"I guess you could say that. My plan was good." Muttered the falcon scratching his great talons. "Look, I'll keep looking. You'd better go with your clan."

Maribel heard more screaming. She looked downstream; the fairy log was going over a giant drop in the river. Maribel pushed the falcon out of the way. "I've gotta go. I've got to rescue that log.

I'm holding you responsible for finding Mimi. You big Oaf!" Maribel pushed hard on the chest of the big bird with her wand.

"Get goin' before I get really mad and do something we'll both regret." Maribel hissed at the bird. "Losing her in a tree. I can't believe it. If you don't find her, I promise you'll deal with me!" She gave the falcon another sharp slap with her wand.

"Ow! I'll find her. I won't be back 'til I do"

Maribel took off with a snap of her wings in the falcon's face. He knew she was furious by her dark purple color and her abrupt lift-off. She shot into the air like a rocket spraying dirt all over him.

CHAPTER 3: HOMELESS

"What do you think that is?" Cadan asked Jaygo, pointing to Mimi. She had her knees pulled up to her chest and was resting her head on them. Her wounded wings were wrapped around her. She was sound asleep. The two elves could only see an oddly shaped dusty gray-blue flower.

"Looks like a dying pansy to me," answered Jaygo. "But how did it get so high in the tree? Let's poke it and see what happens."

Cadan took a long needle from the tree and edged along the branch to the blob of slate blue. He punched the spire like a sword at the lump. He got an immediate, unpleasant reaction.

"OW!" Mimi jumped up into a warrior pose pointing her small wand at them, exposing her full 6 inches, unfurling her short wings. She found herself facing two strange-looking skinny green men, each over twice her size with red hair sticking out from under pinecone hats. They had big, pointed ears rising out the sides of their heads on either side of the cones, hooked noses, and googly eyes. They were wearing tunics made of a leathery substance that barely covered their long arms and even longer legs. Each carried a bow in one hand, a quiver of arrows over their shoulders, and a sword on his belt. The swords were almost as long as Mimi.

Jaygo looked incredulously at Cadan who said, "Jaygo, I think we found one of those fake fairy things. You know we heard about them from Grandma. They fly around close to the ground. But Grandma said they weren't real, just make-believe. Humans make up all kinds of weird stories about them while sitting around the campfire."

The elves' comments made Mimi so angry she color-shifted from pale blue to bright purple. She rose out of her warrior pose to her full height and lowered her wand.

"I certainly am real. I am Princess Mimi LaFae of the Sapphire Clan. I live in the first fig tree inside Bille Park, Paradise. Just exactly who are you weird dudes?" Mimi exclaimed. "Here I'll show you." Mimi struggled taking off her backpack over her sore wings. She finally got it off and started rooting around in it. Finally, she proudly pulled out her half of the medallion and put it over her neck. "See, I have the magic medallion of the Saphire Clan," Mimi told the elves.

"Feisty little thing!" Cadan laughed holding his stomach and shaking all over. As he chuckled, his body went up and down like a yoyo. Mimi thought he must be made of a rubbery substance, maybe silly putty.

"Mimi, that's not exactly a kind way to start introductions when we're twice your size," Jaygo said. "That old thing you just hung on your neck is dirty and missing some decorations. Not exactly royal looking."

"Your pasty blue color doesn't exactly shout royal either," Cadan added. "We'll overlook your rudeness this time since you look beat up and probably aren't showing us your best self. Right, Jaygo?"

Cadan had stopped laughing but still looked skeptically at Mimi. Mimi was staring down at the medallion, gray with soot, and missing some of the gorgeous jewels. The medallion looked like a cheap trinket rather than a magic talisman. The coin was so dull Mimi knew she had no chance of reaching her sister with any vibrations in her half of the medallion. Her only chance of reaching her clan was to hope her sister's half of the medallion was in better condition.

Jaygo added, "I'm Jaygo Treewick and the guy who poked and laughed at you is my brother, Cadan. We're tree elves. It's our job to protect this giant redwood from invasive species. We live in the big burl down there," he said pointing down the tree.

Mimi looked down and saw a huge lump growing out of the tree at least 150 feet below her. "I've heard of elves but I didn't know you were entirely green and stretchy. Mom told me to stay away from you because you're mean to fairies."

"Well, we didn't know fairies were little, tiny unpleasant mites," answered Cadan. "We aren't mean to harmless little creatures. I think you have tree elves and dwarfs mixed up. You want to avoid an angry dwarf. They live underground. You're safe up here." Cadan added, "Instead of thinking of us as the enemy maybe you ought to think of us as rescuers. Looks like you could use some help right now. What are your plans?"

"I got burned in the fire helping Red Robin move her babies. I'm not able to use any of my fairy powers. I can't fly, disappear, or spirit-port my location to my sister. I'm not sure I can even speak bird right now" Mimi said. As she talked, big blue tears rolled down her blue face blotched with big lavender dots from her temper tantrum. "I don't know anyone and I've lost my family," she finished sobbing.

"Well, put that wee stick back in your pack," said Jaygo as he stretched his arms down and out further until they wrapped around Mimi in a sticky hug. "We're sorry honey that you've had such a hard time. We've heard through the cricket call that Paradise is still burning and everything and everyone is gone. You can't go back there."

Cadan interrupted, "Yeh, things are bad. A lot of animals, fairies, birds, and people were killed in the flames. The human houses and forests are all gone. Just black sticks and smoldering piles of ash." He added, "I'm sorry but you're not going to be able to find your family. But we can help you."

"I don't know how. I'm hungry and thirsty. I can't make it down to your house." Mimi answered in a sad little voice.

Cadan said, "No problem. We travel by stretching." He reached his arms up about ten feet to a branch above them, kicking off the branch they were on and swinging all the way around. "Easy, peasy," he finished.

Jaygo added, "And when stretching and swinging doesn't work we jump. See!" He removed his hands from Mimi and jumped to the top of the tree where he leaned out and waved back at them. Now alone on the branch with both tree elves above her, she put her wand back in her pack.

"What a strange world," she thought, "These elves are so different from anything I've seen before. They aren't at all like I was told. They're being nice to me."

Jaygo and Cadan both jumped back down to her branch. Jaygo said, "So let me get this right, your fairy powers aren't working. You can't fly at all, right?"

Mimi nodded her head yes.

Jaygo looked at Cadan and said, "We're going to have to rappel her down to the burl and then your wife can help her with her herb concoctions. What do you think is the easiest way to lower her down?"

Mimi looked down and felt sheer terror. She was used to flying but now she had no idea how she was going to get down with these two tree elves. Cadan stood looking down and then looking back at Mimi.

He snapped his fingers and said, "Got it. She is such a wee mite we'll get a big pinecone. Mimi can sit on it. One of us will hand the cone down to the other. Then the one up above will jump down to a lower branch and we'll do it over again. That way we don't touch her if anything is hurt but we get her down safely."

"Great idea!" Jaygo exclaimed. "Let me go find a cone." Jaygo went springing and swinging away. He was back in a few minutes with a large pinecone. "Cadan help me break off the scales so we can make her a seat." Both elves started breaking off the wooden pieces in the center of the cone.

Mimi wasn't sure she liked this idea at all. She told herself to be brave. She couldn't do anything until she had food and water and felt better. In just a few minutes, the elves had the center of the cone cleared.

Jaygo said, "Can you walk?" Mimi nodded yes.

"Hand me your pack. Come sit here," he said, pointing to the cleared space on the cone.

Mimi edged along the branch and sat in the center of the cone. Jaygo and Cadan were bracing the cone to keep it from falling.

"Ok, you're going to have to hang on tight. We're going to pass you like a hot potato"

Cadan said laughing. "Don't worry. That's a human joke. We

aren't going to throw you. Jaygo, jump down below and I'll pass first."

Jaygo jumped down about ten feet and then stretched his arms up until they were at Mimi's eye level. Cadan leaned out and yelled, "Starting now." He lifted up the cone with Mimi in it and placed it in Jaygo's hands. His hands stretched around the cone and stuck.

Mimi's stomach flipped and she swallowed bile back up her throat. For a second, she was suspended in the air without any support and no wing power.

Jaygo shouted, "Got her." He slowly started lowering Mimi down to his branch. As she was transported down, she felt like she was in a bumpy Ferris wheel starting and stopping.

Mimi saw Cadan jump past her to a branch far below.

Then it was Cadan's turn to reach high, grab, and lower. So the two brothers continued working as a team, with Mimi in the pine cone chair and Cadan and Jaygo jumping, stretching, lifting, and lowering until they got to the giant burl.

Mimi looked back up to where they had started. They had covered over 150 feet in a few minutes without her moving at all. The burl was huge, bumpy, and covered with brown and green moss. The shape was somewhat oblong and it stretched around the tree. There were no doors or windows. Mimi wasn't sure where they were going from here. Cadan stretched out his stringy fingers and helped her out of the pinecone.

Jaygo walked over to a piece of lumpy moss. He lifted it up revealing a round door. A large TW for Treewick was carefully carved in the door. There was also a Christmas tree design. The tree and initials were inlaid with colorful stones. There was a piece of twine hanging by the door. Jaygo pulled on it. Mimi heard what sounded like several tiny sleigh bells ring. The three of them waited a few seconds. The door was opened by a brown field mouse wearing a bright yellow ruffled head piece. The mouse hat looked like an upside-down hollyhock. Her apron was a red maple leaf.

Jaygo said, "Hello, Mrs. Mouse" He then turned to Mimi stretching his arm through the door and into the house, "Miss Mimi, welcome to our home. Let me introduce you to our housekeeper, Mrs. Mouse. She's a field mouse who preferred our home to inclement weather."

"Mrs. Mouse as you can see we have a house guest," said Cadan.

"Can you get her some tea and treats? I believe she is quite hungry."

Mrs. Mouse nodded her head and scurried away on all four legs, her white tail whipping behind her, her apron rustling as she moved.

CHAPTER 4: THE ENCHANTED BURL

The first thing Mimi noticed was the glorious smells that wafted out the open door. There were hints of lavender, mixed with cherry, apple, and cinnamon. Mimi had never been in a nose-friendly house before. Her sense of smell was keen before the fire but had been muted by the smoke.

She breathed in deeply. Happy she was slowly getting some of her skills back.

As she stepped over the threshold, she looked around in amazement. Inside the burl's rough exterior was a glorious wooden pod. She felt like she'd entered a treasure chest. The walls were covered with swirls of orange, brown, and yellow formed by the various knots in the tree... There were windows and skylights covered with a gauzy moss-green substance. The fiber was filmy enough to provide protective cover and sheer enough to let in light.

The house had at least two floors. A wooden spiral staircase wound up to a loft high above. Mimi couldn't see how far back the loft went. The railings of the loft were beautifully carved from pine trees. She didn't know if there were other rooms or additional staircases. The ceiling of the main room was curved. High up in the center were pie-shaped windows laid out in a sphere. The smaller piece of the pie was pointing towards the center. There was a giant round painting of the sky on a clear day featuring a soaring eagle, treetops, and mountains.

The house was filled with glittering treasures. There was a large gold pocket watch hanging from a chain on the wall. A chandelier covered with glittering objects hung in the middle of the pod on several long golden chains. When Mimi looked carefully, she saw the chandelier was a single hoop, possibly a wheel from a bicycle. Small wires of different lengths were displayed on the hoop. There were jeweled and pearl earrings and necklace pendants of different designs. There were golden heart lockets, crystal tear drops, silver charms, and round gemstone pendants. There were even a number of rings. Several looked like diamonds and others were emerald green, light blue, or yellow either semi-precious stones or glass. The jewelry reflected the light from the skylights around the walls making elaborate patterns on the swirling wood. The patterns changed as the light shifted. The chandelier was a focal point in the room brightening the entire spherical space.

The newel post at the bottom of the stairs resembled the beginnings of a large tree with roots growing into the floor. Perched in the post branches was a massive amethyst crystal. A grand round mirror, possibly from a lady's compact, was on the wall. The mirror was decorated with a wreath of dried flowers. Mimi recognized the wall sconces, presently turned off, as head lamps and flashlights of various sizes and shapes.

A wood stove made from a soup can stood in one corner. The can was ventilated out the side of the burl with tin foil. A number of chairs and a large table were intricately carved from wood. There were scenes of trees and forest animals on all the furniture. Pieces of fur and feathers made comfy seats.

Mimi exclaimed, "This is enchanting! One of the most gorgeous homes I've ever been in. Who would think an ugly wood elf could create such beauty?"

"Mimi, you're doing it again. You're making judgments about us without knowing us," Jaygo gently corrected her.

"Oh, I'm so sorry. That just popped out. I seem to have no filter because I'm so tired. We're taught that elves have no skills and are ornery."

Jaygo puffed up his chest and said, "Cadan and I built this house ourselves. Just the best for my family," Jaygo added, "Actually my wife, Karina, designed it. She's a wood woman. Her family roots go back to Scandinavia. She is gorgeous just like this house. You'll meet her soon."

Cadan had come in the door and added, "She and Hannah, my wife, are out scavenging. It's amazing what you can find in the forest. Almost everything in here is things humans left behind and we found and repurposed. We believe in recycling." Cadan added, "My wife is a moss woman whose family is from Germany. She has powerful skills in dealing with herbs. She will be able to help you heal quickly."

Jaygo went over and knelt down to start a fire on the stove. With his back turned, he called over his shoulder, "Cadan, pull that chair over for Mimi to lie on. She's so tiny one of our chairs will be big enough for a bed." He turned back to Mimi and said, "We'll get you settled. Our wives will be back in the blink of an eye."

Jaygo called into the kitchen where Mrs. Mouse was rustling around, "How are you coming with the food, Mrs. Mouse?" There were a couple of squeaks but Mimi didn't speak mouse, only bird so she couldn't understand. "Great!" Jaygo answered.

Cadan pulled up the chair and Mimi gratefully sat down and pulled her legs up, "Thank you."

As soon as Jaygo had the fire going, Mrs. Mouse appeared around the counter that lined the back of the great room carrying a tray with a cup of tea and a huge piece of bread with red jam.

"Here comes Mrs. Mouse with something to take the edge off your hunger," Jaygo added, " We'll feed you more when Hannah tells us what you need to gain your strength back."

"And my powers," Mimi added. "I should have been invisible today but I'm too weak to activate my special powers."

"Lucky for you, we're harmless," Cadan said with a smile.

"More than harmless," Mimi added. "Helpful. Thank you so much for your kindness."

Jaygo had pulled up a small table by the fire as Mrs. Mouse was coming over. She sat the tray down and scurried away. Mimi picked up the teacup, which looked like a thimble with a wire handle attached. She slowly sipped the tea. She savored the warm apple flavor. The tea cured her thirst and eliminated the tickle in her throat caused by the smoke. She broke off a chunk of bread and gobbled it down. With the fire, food, and drink, she started feeling much better and very sleepy.

The next thing she knew Mimi woke up to a woman's laugh. The lights were on and she could hear women's voices chatting quietly at the big table near the kitchen. She stuck her head around the chair to see who was making the noise. Sitting at the table was a gorgeous woman in a skin-tight sparkly brown and black leotard with golden diamond shapes down the back. Mimi looked more closely and recognized the suit as snakeskin. The snakeskin-clad woman had long blond hair braided with flowers.

Giggling with the blonde was a portly, mottled-skinned woman who looked like she was wearing a green/brown camouflage mask. The woman had long dreadlocks and wore a dark green fuzzy pants suit. Mimi realized her skin was that color and thought, "Poor woman, she's so ugly."

The blond was holding up a snake skin. She said, "His loss is my gain. What a great snakeskin belt!"

The other woman laughed and said, "You can highlight it at your tiny waist with the spider broach we found last week." She added, "You put me to shame with your stylish ways. I'm just comfortable in moss weave."

Mimi realized this speaker was Cadan's wife, the Moss woman. So that meant the blond was Jaygo's wife, Hannah the Tree woman. Though both women looked entirely different in size and coloring, they both had distinct pointed ears belonging to the elf race.

Just then Mrs. Mouse scurried in and pointed at Mimi while squeaking loudly. Both women turned and looked right at her.

"Great, the wee one is awake," said the blond.

The one in green said, "She looks terrible. She has dirt and scratches on her face. Her coloring is still a little gray, her dress is in tatters, and her wings are curled."

Mimi wanted to shout, "I'm sitting right here. I can hear you!" She thought, "I must look a mess." She wanted to become invisible but her superpower wasn't working. So instead in a small voice, she said, "Hello!"

The blond leaped out of her chair and landed in front of Mimi.

"Another jumper," Mimi thought. The one with dreadlocks stood up and lumbered over to the chair. While she was moving the blond quickly introduced them, "How rude of us! I'm Karina, Jaygo's wife. Joining us is Hannah, Cadan's wife. Hannah will be able to assess and help you with your injuries. As you can probably tell by looking at her moss clothing, she's a moss woman. The moss people have special healing powers."

Hannah had reached them now and put her large ugly bronze hand on Mimi's shoulder.

Mimi felt warmth flow through her entire body. The heat gave Mimi more energy. Hannah said to Karina, "Poor wee thing. I can tell by her energy she's been through a terrible trauma." Mimi really disliked the way they seemed to talk about her rather than to her. She felt her temperature rising in anger again.

As if Hannah could read Mimi's thoughts, she cooed, "Now wee one, settle down. We don't mean you any harm. You need to save all that heat for healing. I'm just letting Karina know how you're doing."

"We need to get you a bath. Karina can mend your clothing and maybe find you something else to wear," soothed Hannah. Then she touched Mimi's curled wings.

Mimi shouted, "Ouch! That hurts."

"I was afraid of this. Your wings are quite scorched. It is going to take a while for them to heal," said Hannah.

"Will I be able to fly again?"

"Oh, I should think so with the special salve I'm going to mix for you," answered Hannah. "But like any rehabilitation, it's going to take some time and extra effort on your part. Now I want you to rub that purple stone on the staircase every day and concentrate on getting all your fairy spirit powers back. That amethyst is a very powerful stone. It will cleanse your body of any negative energy and help build a protective shield around you."

Karina said, "I'll get Jaygo to set up the spare room." She danced away light as air her reptilian outfit reflecting light. She came back with her arm linked through Jaygo's.

"Honey, can you make up the spare room," she said. "Please." Jaygo leaned over and gave his wife a kiss.

"Of course."

Then he walked over to a wall of the burl that didn't have any decorations and pushed on it. Much to Mimi's amazement the wall stretched out. Jaygo walked into the space and pushed around the wood sides making them wider and taller. Mimi thought it looked like he was playing with clay.

He called back to Karina, "How is this, Honey?"

Karina walked in and looked around. "We need a window up there for light. How about some space over here for a bathroom?"

Jaygo punched out more space for a small, sheltered alcove and then he pushed with all his might to make a hole in the ceiling. Mrs. Mouse came scurrying in pulling a small wagon filled with window coverings, shower curtains, pillows, and a roll-out mat and bedding for sleeping. Cadan showed up wearing a tool belt and started hammering in the bathroom area.

Hannah beamed proudly and said to Mimi, "My husband is quite handy. He's putting in your plumbing."

Everyone stepped out of the newly created room that had light and bedding. Jaygo pulled on the walls some more and made folding doors so Mimi would have privacy.

Karina said to her, "There you go. You now have a room. Go get a shower. Mrs. Mouse has left you some of my smaller clothes. You can put them on for dinner. Hannah will have your salve ready for your wings when you're done with your shower."

"Thank you! Thank you all so much," Mimi said.

"It's nothing," Karina answered. "We want you to rest, get well and be on your way."

Hannah added, "Finding your family is important. As you can see, we are nothing without each other."

Hannah patted Mimi on her shoulder. There was that wonderful warm feeling coming through Hannah's fingers and down through Mimi's body. "Touch the purple crystal, get a shower and we'll see you at dinner." Hannah turned to the rest of the group and said, "Come on let's give her some privacy. We all have things to do."

Once the doors were shut behind her, Mimi checked her medallion. There was no color on it. She tried polishing it. Some of the gray came off but the once brilliant stones looked like rocks rather than jewels. Mimi knew her medallion was not sending out any magical waves. All she could hope for was it would receive a message if Maribel sent one. That assumed Maribel was alive.

CHAPTER 5: A TIME TO HEAL

Mimi had stayed with the Treewick families for five days. During this time, her life had settled into a rhythm. Everyone in the household rose at dawn when the sunlight shone through the gauzy windows. There were lights in the burl at night but limited to the batteries on hand. The entire household was careful to turn lights off when not in use. Ben Franklin's saying, "Early to bed, early to rise," was the motto of the house.

The first morning Mimi found a forest green dress with a gold belt hanging on the door to her room. She didn't recognize the material and rubbed the soft fabric against her face. "Ah, so soft, like velvet," she thought. "But smells fresh like something made from plants."

She later learned at dinner that the dress was created by Karina from fabric made by weaving moss and grass together. The dress went over her shoulders and tied above her wings. When the belt was cinched around her tiny waist, the skirt floated about her legs like a cloud. Mimi thought the green might clash with her blue skin, eyes, hair, and wings but when she put on the dress she felt transformed from a blue fairy to a wood nymph.

Mimi had heard of wood nymphs but had not seen them. In the stories, she'd heard from her Grandma, wood nymphs came from Scotland like her family. They were distant cousins about the same size as her but stayed at the base of oak trees. They were brown and green like the Treewicks and hid among toad stools, mushrooms, and truffles. They had tiny wings that couldn't fly, too small to hold the weight of a nymph. Right now, burned and curled up, Mimi's wings were small and wouldn't hold her.

As the days went on, Hannah treated them with salve every night. Each time Hannah touched her wings, Mimi was surprised by the sweet warmth of Hannah's hands given she was such a big clumsy woman. Hannah worked on the wings, massaging them between her fingers slowly getting them to uncurl.

Mimi did as Hannah directed and rubbed her hands on the purple crystal, morning, and night. When she held onto the crystal, she could feel power coming out seeping down her fingers, and hands and up into her arms. Every day she could feel herself growing stronger.

After rubbing the Amethyst, Mimi would run into her room and rub the medallion with her hands. The grayish tinge slowly melded to copperish gold. The rocks on the coin seemed to be getting more colorful.

This morning when she held the crystal, her fingers and hands disappeared. Mimi was ecstatic. She was getting strong enough to begin hiding in plain sight by becoming invisible. It was one of her most important powers. But she still couldn't mentally call on her invisibility power. She hoped her ability to call up the power for her entire body would return soon. Now if she could just fly.

Every morning Mrs. Mouse set out a bowl of hot porridge and berries for her. Everyone else in the house was already up and gone to their jobs. Mimi never saw Mrs. Mouse until the Treewicks came home at night. There were books in the burl to read to amuse her.

Mainly she spent her time outside building up her strength. She carefully crawled up and down the burl. The wood was scratchy on her knees. Sometimes, she would get a splinter and have to pull it out. She wasn't used to creeping around.

Normally, she would fly but for now, she was stuck on foot. She wasn't sure how to get her wings stronger. She would flutter them back and forth and back and forth to build up their power. Moving her wings was hard. She would stand on a tree limb; close her eyes and say, "Up!" Flapping hard, sweat ran down her face and seeped through her dress. No matter how hard she tried her wings refused to lift her.

Exhausted, she would find a spot in the sun. She could feel the warm glow all over. The warmth helped her control her frustration from her inability to fly. She wanted to scream but didn't want to attract attention. The Treewicks were lovely to her but she belonged with the Sapphire Clan. She was desperate to talk to her sister.

Maybe she thought, "It's the other way around. They're all together and I'm gone. I'm the one who's lost. I wonder if they miss me? Are they sending out search parties? Did they all get burned?"

When Mimi came in from sunning, Mrs. Mouse was racing around the house squeaking and cleaning. Mimi still didn't understand Mouse. But from Mrs. Mouse's frenzied actions, it was clear this was not going to be a normal evening.

Karina skipped in the door a few minutes later, grabbed Mimi's hands, and swung her around in a circle. "Did you hear from the cricket call?" Mimi shook her head no. She didn't understand cricket either. She used to know Bird but her powers were so limited she didn't know if she even knew that.

Karina continued, "The boys have decided we will have a hootenanny tonight. We'll have music and dancing. Mrs. Mouse will whip up something special to eat. Won't you Mrs. Mouse?"

Mrs. Mouse raised her front paws in the air and shook them

crying, "E-eek-eek-E!"

Karina laughed and said, "Oh, Mrs. Mouse, everyone loves your food. Don't worry about the short notice. Stop cleaning. The boys are coming home early to move the furniture. Just work on the food." With that, Mrs. Mouse ran on all fours into the kitchen and Mimi smelled cranberry heating within a few minutes.

The boys, as Karina called Jaygo and Cadan, came in a few minutes later, laughing in deep voices. Jaygo looked at Mimi and said, "Ready to put on your dancing shoes?"

Karina said, "I've told her. Mrs. Mouse is baking."

"Eh, you can smell her cooking a mile away," Cadan said loudly. His comment was obviously heard by Mrs. Mouse because Mimi heard, "eee-EE-y" from the kitchen.

Karina asked, "Where is Hannah?"

"She climbed to the owl perch to invite Professor Owl," Cadan answered.

"Really?" Karina exclaimed. "Only Hannah would be kind enough to personally invite that ole fat feathered creature."

With that, the door swung open, and Hannah thumped in. "Did I hear you two talking about me? Yes, Karina, I did invite Professor Owl and he has decided to join us. He will treat us with his rendition of the *Who Song*."

Both women bent over laughing together. Karina stood back up. She had tears streaming from her eyes. She explained to Mimi, "All that ole owl ever says to us is who."

Jaygo said, "You all have to get dressed. Our guests will be here soon. Cadan and I have to expand the room."

With that, he and Cadan started pushing on the walls of the burl stretching it outward. Hannah stomped and Karina skipped upstairs to their bedrooms.

Mimi went into the guest room. She didn't know what she would wear. But much to her surprise, she found a lacey party dress just her size hanging on the clothes hook. The skirt was white bandage gauze, fixed in layers with a fishing line. The top was embroidered plastic blue carnival beads intermixed with fool's gold sparkling in the sunlight. Sitting below the dress on the floor were small pale blue suede boots with curved toes and princess heels. The women elves, probably Karina, had provided her with a dress fit for any party anywhere in the world. "Oh, how marvelous!" she thought.

Mimi dressed and hurried out of her bedroom. She was now in a giant hall. In one corner, the wood had been pushed up to make a small stage. There were several finches tweeting in the rafters, early arrivals. Jaygo was playing a hand-made wood flute and Cadan was strumming a bass made of a matchbox and rubber bands.

Hannah was wearing a dark green tunic with gorgeous leaves and birds embroidered on it. She had on thigh-high leather boots. A knit headband covered with cheery berries pulled back her dreadlocks.

Karina was wearing a gold strapless pantsuit with a gossamer tail that swished as she moved. Every inch of her suit was covered with elaborate embroidery showcasing parts of the forest. Karina's gorgeous yellow hair was down and pulled back with a rose headband.

Karina was clapping her hands and skipping. Hannah was

stomping her foot. Karina grabbed Mimi's hand and pulled Mimi behind her in a line dance as the music started in earnest.

When the song was over, Mimi looked around. The room now was full of black squirrels, and a variety of birds. There were small bats swooshing through the air and hanging upside down from the beams. There were several wood nymphs just her size dressed in brown with tiny wings. Mrs. Mouse was up on stage hitting a tambourine and dancing a jig. Owl entered filling a large part of the burl. He moved slowly and with great dignity.

Cadan shouted, "Welcome, Professor!" and pointed to a rounded-out part of the burl. Owl slowly proceeded to the space, apparently created just for him. When he got there, the band started again and the air was full of sounds of clapping, stomping feet, the tambourine, woodwind, and bass. Professor Owl's deep voice providing a beat in the background, "Who-o-o, who, who-o-o, who!"

As the evening progressed Mrs. Mouse brought out a huge cake covered with sprinkles. When Hannah cut into it, sprinkles rolled out of the middle across the table and around on the floor. Guests grabbed the cake and stuffed pieces in their mouths. Some guests ran after other guests pushing cake at each other. Soon frosting was all over everyone and all over the burl. Little round candies were rolling around the floor. Everyone was laughing, clapping, stomping their feet, aggressively jumping, bumping, and slamming into each other as they danced. No partners were necessary. The burl was so full of animals and birds that Mimi felt she was in a mosh pit at a concert. The temperature in the burl rose. Mimi was sweaty and she could smell the strange body order of many hot creatures mixing together.

Mimi felt her feet going faster and faster as the music picked up tempo. She started spinning and the next thing she knew she was looking over the crowd. Her little wings were working. She got a little air sick from the height and strange odors. But she was ecstatic to be flying again even if it was just a spin around a burl.

Around midnight Jaygo shouted, "Last song! Thanks for coming."

The crowd hooted and hollered but Cadan and Jaygo quit playing and their guests slowly made their way out the door. As the guests departed Jaygo started pulling the burl back in and Mrs. Mouse started sweeping the mess out the door right behind the guests. By the time Professor Owl stepped outside, the burl was back to normal size and there were no signs that a huge hootenanny had taken place.

Mimi looked down. She was still dressed up, so she hadn't been dreaming. She was exhausted, had frosting on her clothes and her armpits were sweaty. She thanked the Treewicks for their hospitality and threw herself on her bed fully clothed.

CHAPTER 6: EVACUATE

Mimi awoke to an unusual noise in the forest, human racket. Machines growled through the trees and male human voices shouted out directions. The first thing she thought was, "Danger!"

She got out of bed and peeked out a window. There were two men on a four-wheeler zipping towards her. They stopped at the Treewick Tree and got off.

The one wearing a red baseball cap pointed at the burl and exclaimed, "Isn't she a beaut!"

The other with a black beard and plaid cap, held up binoculars and walked around the bottom of the tree. When he got back, he said, "Absolute stunner Not an imperfection on that burl."

"Ok, let's mark it," said the first man. The second man got out a bucket of paint and brush. He opened the can and painted a big orange x on the tree. Mimi almost started crying. But she had to be still. She didn't want to attract the humans' attention. An orange x was the mark of death for a tree. It meant the humans planned on cutting it down.

When he was done with the mark, the man with the beard asked, "When do you think they'll come get it?"

The red-capped driver said, "Oh, probably Friday, Monday at the latest. I can't wait to see the inside of that burl. I bet it has gorgeous designs. It's one of the biggest I've ever seen. We ought to name it Big Boy!"

The bearded man waved his hand as he exclaimed, "Imagine the lace and feathers lining Big Boy. What fabulous table tops it'll make! We ought to get a fortune for it. I'd say in the thousands for sure."

The two men climbed back on their four-wheeler and roared off towards more trees. Mimi heard one of them say, "Jack, told me to go over the rise. There's another big burl over there but nothing like this one."

****

Hannah, Cadan, Jaygo, and Karina all came in together. Hannah was crying. Cadan comforted her by putting his arm across her broad shoulders.

Karian was talking quickly in an angry voice, "I can't believe we have to move again. We've only been here six months."

Jaygo tried to soothe her, "You know we've moved before. We can do it again."

"But they just keep finding us. You and Cadan build gorgeous burls and burl hunters come after us." Karian wailed.

Cadan turned to Mimi and asked, "Did you see the orange x?" Mimi nodded her head yes.

"You know those thieves have targeted our burl for destruction?" Mimi pierced her lips in a frown and nodded again.

"I heard the men at the foot of the tree this morning," she answered.

Hannah interrupted in a tearful voice, "We can't stay. We keep having to move because they cut out our burls and then sell them. Cutting out the burl is like cutting out the heart of the tree. Once the tree is gone, the moss goes too. Without moss, there is nothing to hold the water. Soon everything is gone. The humans have a name for it, 'Clear Cut,' Hannah finished in disgust.

Cadan added, "We're tree elves. We can't exist without a tree. If they destroy our home before we find another they kill us."

"You have until Monday," Mimi said. "At least that's what I heard."

The four tree elves looked at each other. "Well, that gives us more time than last time," Jaygo said. "We need a better plan. Last time we just hurried over the hill to get a home started in time to stay alive."

Cadan added, "We need to go to one of those areas the cricket call told us about. We need to find a national park with Redwoods."

Jaygo snapped his fingers and said, "Righto! I remember now. The humans aren't allowed to cut down trees in the national park."

Hannah wiped her eyes and looked hopeful, "But how do we find one of those? Can we get to one in time to save our souls?"

Cadan said, "I know how to find one. We'll visit the gypsy in the forest. She's been all over. I bet she has a map or magic cards to get us there."

"Good thinking. I know the answer to the second question. Once we find out where we're going, we'll plan a course. We may have to build smaller burls along the way to keep us safe, We can be in our escape burl by Monday."

"But we've made this our home, and it's so beautiful," Kariana interjected,

"We built this home, We can build another," Jaygo reassured her "Think of wee Mimi over there. Her home is totally gone and she isn't with any family or friends. We have the four of us to make this work."

Mimi was upset when she heard Jaygo's words. "What about me?" she asked. "Am I going with you?"

Cadan answered, "That's a tough question, Mimi. We can't leave you here in a burl that's getting cut down. You don't travel like us. You know that, stretch and swing. You aren't flying. You're too tiny to leave alone."

Mimi realized she was crying now.

Hannah put her warm hands on her shoulders. Mimi felt peace flow through her. "Don't worry little fae. We won't leave you without a plan," Hannah said calmly. "Jaygo, what are we going to do?"

"I think we'll do two things. We'll send out a message on cricket call and see if we can find out if any of Mimi's family and friends are alive. I should have done that as soon as she arrived but I didn't think she was up to any bad news." He turned to Mimi, "Sorry if you think I didn't do the right thing."

"What's the second idea?" asked Karina.

"We'll all go to the gypsy. We'll ask her what she thinks Mimi ought to do. She knows magic and how to tell the future. She can tell us if Mimi should go with us, stay put, or travel some other way."

"Right now, you aren't sure what's happening to me," Mimi sniffled through a tissue.

"For sure, we know you aren't going to be left here alone to deal with humans," Cadan said. "You can stop worrying. Jaygo's good with putting plans together and the rest of us are really good at working together."

Karina looked over and saw Mrs. Mouse standing in the kitchen holding her apron up to her nose. "I'm sorry Mrs. Mouse," Karina said. "But you and I both know that you can't go with us. You'll have to go back to your family in the field. We've loved sharing our home with you."

"OK it's settled," Jaygo said, "We'll see the gypsy and be in a safe temporary place by Monday. Mimi, we'll get a plan for you. Mrs. Mouse, you'll go back to your family."

Hannah looked around with sad eyes and said, "I love you all so much! Everybody together for a group hug."

The tree elves, the field mouse, and the fairy all came together in a group. Jaygo's and Cadan's stretchy arms pulled them tight together and Hannah's warm hands made everyone feel better, not so alone.

CHAPTER 7: GYPSY FORTUNE TELLER

"What is that thing?" Mimi whispered to Karina.

Hannah petted a giant grey rabbit with prone horn antlers growing out of his head. He had his head bent down to her height. She was whispering in a giant floppy ear. Mimi and Karina stood too far away to hear the conversation.

"That's Jack, short for Jackalope," Karina answered. "He's exceedingly rare. His ancestors are jack rabbits and antelopes. Fearsome in battle folks say."

"I've never seen one," Mimi answered. She admired Jack's beautiful grey fur, soft as a down blanket.

"He's not from around here. Jackalopes are from Wyoming and the open plains," Karina explained. "We're not sure how he got here. He doesn't talk. Hannah found him badly injured, a gash in his side. She stitched up the wound and healed him with her special mixture of mud and herbs. He'll come to her when she whistles. He seems to understand what she says."

As Hannah kept whispering, the rabbit said nothing. He shook his head "No." Hannah whispered more fervently this time. She pointed west through the forest. In the background, the noise of the human four-wheelers and electric saws started up. Both Hannah and Jack stopped and looked up at the noise. Jack stood on his hind legs and sniffed in the air. He was about a foot taller than Hannah. Hannah whispered some more to Jack while pointing towards the noise. She clutched his fur with both hands as if begging. The rabbit finally gave a small nod up and down in a "Yes."

"Oh, thank goodness!" Karina exclaimed. "He's agreed to take us."

"We're getting on that great hairy beast?" Mimi asked.

Hannah was waving them over. "Yes, not a minute to lose," Karina said, pushing Mimi forward. "You heard the humans in the woods behind us. We must get away to safety before they kill our tree. Do you have all your gear?"

Mimi nodded. She was carrying her backpack, wearing a slim shaggy brown long-sleeved shirt and brown pants. The pants and shirt were as soft as velvet. Hannah had woven them for her from moss and grass. Except for her blue skin, she could have been mistaken for a member of the Brownies.

"Yes, isn't it exciting?" Karian exclaimed. "A ride on a giant wild animal"

Hannah hurried over and lifted Mimi's pack. "Let's go! No time to loiter. Where are the boys?"

At that moment, Jaygo and Cadan swung down from the trees and landed by the women. "So are we set?" Cadan asked. "Will the great beast carry the three of you to the gypsy's wagon?"

"Your wife has a way with animals, as you well know. She tamed you didn't she." Katrina joked. "The answer is yes. Jack will take us at least as far as the gypsy. We're off on a grand adventure."

"That's one way to look at it," Jaygo said. "Or you could focus on the fact that we're running for our lives from the most dreaded beast on earth, humans."

"Let's go. You two take to the trees. And the three of us will load up on Jack. We'll see you at the gypsy's. You said she was at the fourth oak at the bend in the road. Is that right?" Hannah asked.

Cadan quickly kissed his wife, "Righto, we're off to the canopy." With that, Jaygo and Cadan swung up into the nearest tree and stretched forward, moving at a rapid pace.

Hannah looked at the other two women and said, "Well, get over here and meet Jack. He's not going to wait around all day. He's a wild hare." Hannah was petting Jack and talking to the other two over her shoulder. "Don't call him a rabbit. That is a terrible insult. A hare has longer legs and ears than a rabbit. Jack's a powerful member of the Jackalopes, very few hares have horns."

All three were now standing by Jack. When Hannah patted him on the shoulder he lay down. Hannah turned to Mimi and said, "You're the smallest so I'm going to push you up and then you scooch back to just before Jack's butt, Karina you go in the middle, and I'll ride up front to give directions. Give me your foot." Hannah directed Mimi. Mimi lifted her dainty foot into Hannah's outstretched hand and Hannah tossed her up and forward.

"Whoa," Mimi thought, reaching out desperately for fur. She found herself on Jack hanging off the far side. "Sorry, a little hard," Hannah apologized. "You ok?"

"I'm hanging onto fur and climbing," Mimi called from the other side of the hare. She started scrambling up Jack's side to his back. He turned and gave her a dirty look. She realized for the first time that he had razor-sharp teeth. "Sorry, Mr. Jack!" Mimi exclaimed. "I'm up." She shouted to the other two as she moved back on Jack's back.

Karina's mount was much more graceful. She was, of course, much taller than Mimi so that helped. Hannah lifted her up and Karina stretched a leg across Jack. Mimi blew out a breath in frustration. Everything Karina did was done with grace. Mimi felt like a nat.

Hannah moved far back. She bent down into a racing position and then started lumbering at full speed at Jack. Mimi was horrified. She was sure Hannah would slam hard into Jack and everyone would be thrown off. Just as Hannah reached Jack's side, Jack scrunched down further and Hannah jumped with all her might, arms up, hands extended, and managed to grab the rough of his neck. Hannah kicked her legs and pulled with her arms and Karina grabbed the back of Hannah's belt and pulled too. Hannah threw a leg over Jack and they were all loaded up.

Hannah looked back with a smile and ordered, "Hang on tight ladies!" She kicked Jack in the side and leaned forward shouting "Go Jack." They all sailed into the air. Mimi was sitting on nothing. She was just swinging behind Karina. Fortunately, since her wings were slowly healing, she could flap them to provide ballast and stay with the group. Karina was screaming with glee as if she were on a carnival ride. Hannah was bent forward like a jockey on a racehorse, giving encouragement to Jack. Between Karina's squealing and focusing on staying on, Mimi couldn't see where they were going or hear what Hannah was saying.

The next thing Mimi knew, the hare hit the ground with a hard thump and then propelled them forward. The undulating motion was relentless, thump, propulsion thump again. Mimi started to lose her ballast as Jack turned right. "Must be the bend in the road," Mimi thought. She counted one oak. Thump, push. Thump push. A second oak. Swinging further right. Thump, push, thump push. Another oak. Thump push, thump push. STOP! Mimi slammed into Karina. Her long blue hair flew over her face. When she flipped it back, she was staring at a small red wagon with a round canvas top. An olive-skinned woman with black hair tied back by a colorful scarf was sitting on the top step of the wagon.

The woman was dressed in a red gathered skirt and white blouse with puffed sleeves. A white pony was grazing near the wagon. The woman was puffing on a pipe. Circles of smoke rose in the air.

"Took you long enough to get here," the woman said as a way of welcoming. "Jack here is getting slow in his old age."

Jack snorted and showed his teeth.

"Oh, put those fangs away ole boy," ordered the woman. "You know you're not going to use them on Rosella. Where are the green munchkins?" the woman asked. Hannah looked up in the trees and Jaygo and Cadan dropped down. Hannah slid off Jack dragging Katrina and Mimi behind. Both Katrina and Mimi landed on their butts.

"Hey! A little notice next time," Katrina snapped at Hannah.

"I saw you were coming in the cards. I've been waiting for you." Rosalla said. "Come in and we'll see where you're headed. That's why you came to me, isn't it? To see where to go?"

Hannah spoke for the group, "Rosella, we are so thankful you would see us without notice. We are desperate. Humans are ripping the soul out of our tree."

"I know. I saw everything in my globe. My globe shows me what is going on when directed but doesn't read the future. For that, I have to use my psyche earth cards," explained Rosalla. "We have to identify your destination and find a spirit animal to accompany you. No time to waste. Come on in."

Mimi was fascinated. She had never dealt with a Gypsy before and wasn't sure of their special powers. She didn't know about magic globes and cards. She was excited to see them.

The four elves and Mimi tromped into the small wagon. Hannah turned to Jack as she was entering and said, "Jack wait." Jack lay down at Hannah's command. Mimi at first thought they wouldn't all fit in the small space, but the wagon seemed to expand. Mimi wasn't sure if it was an optical illusion or magic.

The wagon was entirely draped in red curtains. There was no outside light coming in.

Rosella waved at the curved benches around a small round table and said, "Sit down."

As she settled in, Mimi noticed there was a small round globe in the middle of the table. The globe started glowing and Mimi saw a small figure appear. The figure was a white-haired woman. She had glorious wings. and blue skin. Mimi leaned in closer. She stared astounded. She cried out, "That looks just like Maribel! I have to talk to her. I have to get to her."

Mimi pounded on the glass ball with her fist and started shouting, "Maribel." Failing to get her attention, she pulled back and ran as hard as she could at the ball slamming into it and knocking herself back on her butt.

Rosella shouted, "Grab her! She'll break the ball." Mimi felt long green arms stretching around her and pulling her back.

"I have to get to Maribel! Let me go."

"Oh stop it, you silly girl. The ball shows you the present. You can't communicate with it. Sometimes knowing what is happening to those you care about helps you plan."

Tears were running down Mimi's face, "I have to get to Maribel."

"Well, you won't do it by smashing in the ball," Rosella replied in a soothing low voice. "All you'll do is make a big gooey wet mess and possibly kill yourself on the broken glass. Why don't you settle down and we'll start with our elf friends? The good news is we know that your sister, Maribel is alive."

Rosella placed long knarled fingers around the crystal ball. Her blood-red nails were about an inch long and reached almost around the ball. Inside the ball, Mirabel disappeared into a gray mist. The ball started glowing and radiating heat. The wagon went totally black and started shaking like an earthquake. Lightening spears shot from the ball. Mimi was terrified and wanted to hide under a cushion or run away. But the others sat very still staring at the ball.

Seconds later, full light returned. Rossella lifted her hands revealing a hazy white cloud filling the ball, like a delicate frothy meringue. Rosella closed her eyes and placed her hands back on the ball. The white lifted like a fog clearing. The magic burl came into view. Far down the tree line, men with chain saws were cutting down trees. Rosella placed her hands back on the ball and a heart came into view.

Rosella looked up at Hannah and said, "You have brought the heart of the tree with you?" Hannah nodded. "That's marvelous. We have a place to begin. All we must do is find where the tree spirits want you to take the heart. If you follow that pathway, you will be able to create a safe new home."

CHAPTER 8: THE ELFIN WAY

Rosella looked at Hannah and said, "I can tell you are by far the most intuitive in the group. You are a healer, right?" Hannah nodded. "Then you will work with me in selecting the cards that will tell you where to go and interpreting them." Rosella pulled out a small wooden box with intricate designs of woodland animals in a forest and placed it on the table. She opened the box. Inside was a forest green silk scarf wrapped around a rectangle. When she unrolled the scarf, Mimi saw Rosella was holding colorful cards. On the back of each card was the same woodland scene.

Rosella handed the cards to Hannah, "Use your mind to focus on your journey. Tell the cards that you want to travel safely to a new place. Ask them where to guide you." As Hannah was holding the cards, Rosella looked at the other four and said, "These are Magic Earth cards. No two cards are the same. The cards are an infallible oracle telling you what to do. Your job is to concentrate and read them correctly. I am an expert reader but even I have failures because people like you do not focus... All of you should be helping Hannah." Rosella placed her hands over Hannah's and the cards. She asked, "Where should the elves go next?"

Mimi watched as a golden arch circled Hannah's hand. Rosella murmured, "This is good, very good." She looked up at Hannah, "You have an extraordinarily strong connection to the goodness of the earth. Very few people can create the positive energy that leads to the arch. I'm sure the cards will give you faithful advice. Now place them on the table."

Hannah did as she was directed. Rosella spread the cards out. So far all the cards still looked the same, with trees like a forest with animals. "Draw any three cards that speak to you," Rosella directed Hannah.

Hannah raised her mottled green-bronze hand and passed over the cards once. Mimi realized she was holding her breath to see what Hannah would draw. She forced herself to take a couple of deep breaths.

Hannah pointed at one card at the beginning. Rosella pushed it face down towards her. She picked another near the end. Again, Rosella pushed it towards her. Finally, after making several more passes with her hand, Hannah picked the last card. Rosella lined the 3 cards up in front of Hannah.

"Now turn them over and your destiny will be revealed."

The first card was a pile of brightly painted redwood. Hannah turned over the second card. There was a picture of the rolling waves, a sandy beach, and huge trees rising behind the sand. Now Mimi did hold her breath waiting for the third and final card. Hannah pulled it slowly towards her and flipped it. There was a Native American man wearing a wolf skin head band on his forehead. The head band was decorated with eagle feathers. The man wore rows and rows of necklaces made from rounded pearl seashells and a deerskin apron. He held a large fish in his hand. There was a woven basket at his feet. Mimi was at a loss as to what these three cards could mean. How could they provide direction for her elf friends to move on in safety?

Rosella looked at Hannah and slowly smiled revealing crooked teeth with a gold front tooth. "You have done well, my dear. You have found a permanent home for you and the tree's soul you protect."

"What does it mean?" asked Hannah.

"Ah, the cards speak clearly if you understand them. What do you see in the first card?"

"A stack of redwood."

"Correct. What is the largest tree in the forest, the giant redwood?"

Jaygo interrupted, "But we've lived in redwoods before and we are searching for a new home. Why should we think they would be safe?"

Rosella stared at him with blazing black eyes. "The cards do not lie. They capture your destiny if you believe and read them correctly. What does the second card say to you, you wanker?" she asked Jaygo angrily.

Jaygo stared at it a moment and said, "It's a picture of the sea rolling in towards the forest."

"Correct. So, you are to head west towards the sea where the giant redwoods grow. But the third card is the most important." Rosella turned back to Hannah, "What do you see girl? You are clearly the bright light among this group?"

"I see a Native American man in full regalia. But I am not familiar with the tribe."

"But I am. You can tell by his tall eagle feathers and wolf head band that he belongs to the Yoor-ock tribe. They have honored and protected the redwood for hundreds of years. They have been pushed out of the redwood forests by white men, but they still cherish the trees. They are north of the Klamath River. If you head west and north, you will find protected forest. You will be safe for many years. Hopefully, many generations."

"But how do we get there?" asked Cadan.

"You travel as you came. The men swing and walk. The women take Jack. Tell Jack to go easy since you, Hannah are with child."

"Really?" Hannah exclaimed. She looked at Cadan with wonder. "We so want little ones."

"Well, you have one. It is early days and you must travel with care. But Jack likes you and is reliable. He will defend you with his life. I am also sending along my wolf. Fenrir come."

From under a window seat, a giant white wolf rose and sat by Rosella. Mimi was terrified and fascinated by his beauty. He had gray flecks interwoven in his fur. In the light from an upper window, his coat resembled sparkling frost. His eyes were the palest blue. He turned his head and stared at Mimi. His eyes seemed almost white. She felt like he was looking through her. He seemed as big as a small pony. Yet no one had noticed him in the very small wagon until Rosella had called him.

"Don't worry, Fenrir is quite gentle to those I tell him to protect. He's also quite fearsome to those intent on harm. He was born on the Yoor-ock reservation. Getting there is imprinted in his brain."

"But how can you give him to us? You and he obviously have a spiritual bond," asked Cadan.

"Oh, I'm not giving him to you. I'm asking him to lead the way. No one owns Fenrir. He's a lone wolf. He shares my love of the earth. I have no doubt that after you find a tree to be the home of your tree heart, he will return to me. That is his choice. Never forget you must trust Fenrir. He only serves those who honor him."

Jaygo asked, "So do we just go behind him? How do we build his trust?"

Rosella reached for a medallion hanging down her neck on a piece of string. She lifted it over her head and showed it around the room. The medallion was a silver wolf's head with sharp teeth and a diamond for an eye. When she passed it by Fenrir. He sniffed at it and made a low growl. Rosella patted him on the head. "Don't worry boy. No one is in trouble yet."

Rosella turned to Jaygo and said, "Wear this medallion at all times. This is the precious totem of the wolf tribe. The medallion provides a bond between you and Fenrir. It also links you to the Yoor-ock tribe. The chiefs had it made of pure silver to honor the wolf. If you are in trouble, hold it firmly in your hands and call for Fenrir. He will always hear you and come. As you travel, rub the medallion and ask it to guide you."

Rosella turned to Fenrir and directed firmly, "Go with the elves. Take them to Klamath Falls, the home of your brothers and sisters. Keep them safe." The wolf stared at Rosella and growled in a low voice as if agreeing.

"Now give your little blue friend a hug and say your goodbyes," directed Rosella as she pointed at Mimi.

"What?" shrieked Mimi.

"Girl, it's simple. You aren't going with them. You weren't meant to live in a magic burl. Your destiny is with your sister you tried to beat out of the glass."

"I don't understand," Mimi cried.

Rosella spoke to her as if she were speaking to a spoiled child,

"Your elfin friends' destiny is in the northern California redwoods.

We haven't looked for your destiny yet. You act like a simpleton. You are meant to find your sister and your fairy clan."

Hannah leaned over and pulled Mimi to her heart. "Don't worry little one. Rosella will have a plan for you."

Cadan patted Mimi on the head, "We must go, Mimi. We give you our love and blessings, but we have to get our tree heart to a new home before ours is destroyed and our souls extinguished."

Jaygo patted her head too and said, "You'll do great. You're the feistiest fairy I've ever had the pleasure to meet."

Mimi stomped her foot and answered, "I'm the only fairy you've ever met."

"That's true," Jaygo answered with a smile. "But you've been a fierce wee one from the moment we met you."

Karina shook her head no at Jaygo and scolded "Don't tease. She's scared, hurting." Then she leaned down and kissed Mimi on the cheek, "Wish us well my little friend. I promise to seek you out once we have a new home and you are settled. Send word by the eagle call."

After saying goodbye to Rosella, the four elves and Fenrir stepped out of the wagon. Mimi peaked out the door. Jaygo was rubbing the medallion and looking west as Hannah helped Karina on Jack's back. Jaygo looked at the women once they were on the jackalope's back and asked, "All ready?"

Hannah gave a thumbs up as Karina hung on for dear life. Fenrir was pacing in a circle nearby. Jaygo called out to Fenrir, "Take us to the Yoor-ock tribe." Fenrir sat down and smelled the air. Then he made a wild howl that echoed through the forest and took off at a run. Jaygo and Cadan stretched up into the trees to follow him. Jack started leaping at an amazing speed. In a few seconds, all Mimi could see was the dust from Jack's departing hind feet.

Mimi was alone again.

CHAPTER 9: MIMI FINDS HER WAY

Rosella came back into the wagon after sending the others off. She found Mimi sitting on the table staring at an empty crystal ball with silent tears running down her face. "We don't have time for your hysterics right now. Are you crying for your friends traveling to safety or the young woman in the ball?"

"Both. I'm alone again. I don't know when I'll ever see either the elves or Maribel again."

"Let's talk about this Maribel. Who is she to you? Before you arrived, the ball showed me half an old tarnished medallion. The intricate design was of a giant fig tree with a leaf canopy and long roots. Do you have this medal?"

"Oh yes," answered Mimi excitedly. She hurried to her backpack and pulled out the dirty medal.

"Let me hold it," directed Rosella. Mimi handed the piece to her.

"I always carry it with me. That was why I had to have my backpack when I left Cyan Castle fleeing the fire."

"I can feel the heat in this piece. You must be very important to your clan to be allowed to carry such a valuable piece." Rosella stared carefully at Mimi with her very black eyes. She studied her for what seemed like hours but was probably only seconds. "I can see now. Your injuries keep you from presenting yourself as the powerful fairy you are. You are a leader of your people. But you are missing half of your power. Does this Maribel have the other half of the medallion?

Mimi was surprised by how perceptive Rosella was. But when she thought about it, why wouldn't Rosella know something about

Maribel? Afterall, she'd seen her trapped in the glass globe on her table. "I'm not a leader. I'm just Maribel's follower. She's my older sister and the leader."

"Tell me about your sister."

"Maribel is the leader of the Sapphire Clan. I'm her protector. Our ancestors the Sapphires from Scotland fled the fairy extermination by the infamous black trolls. The entire clan travelled together across vast seas sailing over the North Pole in a wooden boat. My great, great-grandparents arrived safely in the new land with sunny blue skies, abundant wildlife, plants, and trees. They pledged to always take care of the clan in the new land. To keep danger like the trolls away they made the medallion. A very powerful spell was put on it by a wizard. They split the medallion in half so no one could steal it. Also, they didn't want one person in the clan to have too much power. By splitting the coin power is shared. I'm not very important but my sister is."

"I can feel the power in this medallion and yet here you sit. Wounded and alone. Why don't you call on it instead of coming to me?"

"Because the medallion only works when interlocked with the other half. Maribel has that half. Maybe you saw it on her neck. She always wears hers. When they link together, the magic of the clan is doubled. But without the connection, the medallions are useless. When they link the colors and energy is amazing."

"I see," said Rosella. "You two are like Siamese twins. When you are separated you can function but part of you is missing. So you would like to find this Maribel?"

"Oh yes, please help me find her," pleaded Mimi. "I'm sure most of the remaining Sapphires are with her."

"I can see you are still recovering from the fire." Said Rosella.

"Yes, my wings were singed. I haven't been able to fly. I'm finally getting where I can do a few upward propulsions." Mimi pointed at her backpack and said in a small sad voice, "My twisted wand has been useless since the fire. Hannah had some special herbs. She rubbed salve on my wings every night. But my healing has been slow. I don't know if my personal magic powers will ever return."

"Well now I understand you are a lost princess in search of her sister and clan. I know what we must do. Let's begin by asking the gazing ball to tell us what is going on with your sister. Remember, the ball is only a vision. You mustn't touch it or make noise. Whatever or whoever we see cannot hear us. The images in the ball don't know we are looking in."

Rosella placed her long fingers around the ball. She squeezed until her blood-red nails almost touched. Her fingers turned white from the pressure. The colors in the globe changed from clear to grey and finally foamy white. As the foam dissipated an image of a glorious royal blue fairy in a silver flight uniform waving huge iridescent wings emerged. No noise came from the glass. The fairy was twisting and turning shooting laser beams from her straight blue wand. Maribel was clearly in a battle. The enemy was not visible in the globe. As Maribel waved the wand sharp points of light shot outwards. Red splashed on the inside wall of the globe. Gray filled the globe and the image disappeared.

"What happened?" shouted Mimi. "Is she alright?"

"We don't know," Rosella answered calmly. "We know she is alive. She's in a battle but we don't know where or with whom."

She added with a sly look, "She's certainly a striking young woman."

"I know. I don't look like her. I'm tiny, shy, and weak. But I must try to help her. She's very powerful but I know I could help. I pledged to help when I took the medallion."

"That may not be destiny's calling for you child. You need to draw your cards to see what your future holds. At least you know, right now Maribel is alive. From the looks of it, unharmed. She looked like a great warrior."

Rosella pulled out her cards and handed them over to Mimi. "You're too small to hold them so sit on them."

Mimi leaped up on the pack with the help of her wings. She thought to herself, "Thank goodness I'm beginning to jump and fly a little."

"Ask them to tell you what to do and where you should go. Clear your mind. Focus on the cards, not on Maribel or your elf friends. This is about you. Ask what you should do."

Mimi sat on the deck with her legs folded and her hands covering her eyes. She said to herself, "Tell me what to do next. I'm lost right now and need to know where to go."

"Now get off the deck and point to the cards you want me to pull for you."

Mimi dropped down to the table and stood next to the deck of cards. She pointed at the bottom one. Rosella pulled it out and turned it over. There was a picture of a white church with a steeple and doors open.

"What can that mean?" said Mimi. "Am I supposed to go to

church?"

"Let's not be hasty in analyzing what the cards are telling you.

You need to pull two more and then I will read them for you." Mimi pointed to a card in the middle of the deck.

Rosella pulled the card out and turned it over. There was a picture of three beautiful girls of different sizes who had a family resemblance. "Ah, you have chosen the three sisters. Interesting," said Rosella. "Pull your last card."

Mimi pointed to a card near the top of the deck.

Rosella pulled the card and flipped it over. There was a bend in the road. "You have drawn a church, three sisters, and a bend in the road. The cards are telling you to seek sanctuary."

"But I have to go to Maribel."

"No, you don't. You are not fully healed and if you are able to find Maribel you may be a burden to her. She is clearly fighting, and she would have to protect you. You are to seek safety and if it is your destiny to be with Maribel, she will find you."

"But where am I to go?" asked Mimi a little tearfully.

"The Three Sisters are volcanic peaks in Oregon. I traveled there this summer. Bend is a town near the Three Sisters. The cards are telling you to seek sanctuary in Bend, Oregon. Your elfin friends are traveling west and north. You will need to travel north."

"How am I going to travel? My wings are just starting to work. My twisted wand has little power. It needs to be fully recharged."

"You must go to Wizard Island at Crater Lake on your journey.

The island is where all Wizards recharge when they are burned out and in need of recharging. If you can get to the island your wand and wings will be repaired."

"You can travel on a javelina I've been keeping out back. A hunter came through a few days back and gave me Joseph. He was in exchange for a card reading. I was planning on eating him but I'm sure he'd rather take you north.'

"But I have no idea how to get there."

"I'm going to send Ravina my Raven with you too. She has a wonderful sense of direction." At that moment, a black bird sitting on a tall pole in the corner cawed. Mimi had thought the bird was stuffed it had been so quiet. "You may remember that Noah sent a raven out to find land. We'll send Ravina to find Bend. Come here Ravina," Rosella said. The raven flew from the pole to Rosella's shoulder. "Ravenia show Mimi how you give directions."

The ravin raised her head, flapped her wings, and let out a huge "Cawwww!"

"You'll need to make Joseph follow Ravina's call. Your wand should work well as a small electric prod to get him to do your bidding. We can practice before you leave."

"Maybe if we practice, I can make this work. I've never seen a javelina. Are they trained and easy to ride?"

Rosella laughed, "Oh no. They are quite wild. They don't belong here. They live in the southwest. They certainly don't live up north but I'm sure you two will get along fine. If you don't, I'm sending a little friend to keep you company. I like you. I'm going to give you one of my favorite pets, Chatty Cathy to keep you company." Rosella pulled an African pygmy hedgehog out of her skirt. "Meet Chatty."

The hedgehog started talking right away, "How are you? I'm Chatty Cathy. What's your name? Where are you from?" Rosella popped the hedgehog back in her pocket. There were small garbled noises and then silence. "The best way to shut up Chatty is to put her away. I'd suggest you keep her in your backpack."

"I took her from a customer in payment because she was sooo cute. To be perfectly honest her senseless chatter is getting on my nerves. But you have a long journey and someone to talk to might be nice. Remember she really has nothing to add to the conversation."

"Thank you, I think," Mimi said hesitantly. She wasn't sure a tiny talking hedgehog with nothing to say was going to be helpful.

She thought, "Well, at least I'll have company. She is cute and apparently harmless."

"You seem to have everything arranged," said Mimi in a small voice.

"That's why folks come to me to find answers," Rosella said proudly, sitting up straight and smiling. Her gold tooth protruded again. "Let's go outside and meet Joseph."

Rosella scooped up Mimi and put her on her shoulder. As she exited the wagon, Rosella had Ravenia on one shoulder, and Mimi on the other. She took Chatty out of her pocket. The little voice started, "Oh, we're going on an adventure. How exciting. I get to come right? Right?"

Rosella lifted Chatty Cathy up looked her in the eye and said, "Right. You're leaving me now. I've had enough of your cuteness."

Outside Rosella let out a high sharp whistle. Mimi heard a

rustling around in the bushes on her right. There was a high-pitched crying sound like a baby. Then an animal that looked something like a pig but had a long snout and fangs scampered out of the coyote brush. He was reddish with gray and white hair. He had a black Mohawk down his neck.

"Sit," Rosella directed. The creature sat. Mimi was shocked by how ugly he was and by how big he was. She had thought Jack, the jack-a-lope, was hard to ride with Hannah and Karina helping. Guiding this beast on her own seemed impossible.

"Ok," said Rosella. "I'm going to tie a scarf around Joseph's neck, just as a precaution. You can always hang onto his ruff. But if you get in trouble you can grab the scarf." She pulled a gorgeous large purple scarf out of her pocket. The silky square was the color of ripe grapes in the fall. In the center was a huge golden triangle filled with tiny peacocks and tangerine-colored paisley swirls. Mimi was shocked. How could Rosella wrap such a glorious creation around such a despicable beast? Rosella leaned down and tied the scarf around Joseph's neck like a bandana with a bow on his neck. "Good Boy," she said patting Joseph on his head. Joseph looked like he was wearing a fancy bib to eat lobster at an elaborate dinner party.

"Mimi, you are going to have to make Joseph mind you. Use your wand. He looks quite mild right now but he can run up to 35 miles an hour and has been known to kill and eat dogs." Mimi cringed inside. She was just getting back the use of her wand powers and hoped it would work to prod Joseph. "Now I am assuming your wings work well enough to help you get on and off him. He's about two feet tall. I can put you on him now to practice but I won't be with you on the trip. I'm going to put you on the ground and see if you can lift yourself up."

Rosella bent over and placed Mimi next to Joseph. He looked

down at her curiously and smelled her with his ugly fanged snout. Mimi gagged when she smelled a strong sweet odor coming from the beast. "What is that smell?" she cried out as tears ran down her cheeks. She put her hand over her mouth to keep from throwing up.

"Oh that, it's nothing. Javelinas have a scent gland on their back. People say you can smell a heard coming before you see them. The smell is harmless. I can see since it's turned your lovely blue color a little green that you don't like it too much."

"It's awful." Mimi cried.

"You're so whiney" scolded Rosella. "You'll get used to it. In fact, you'll probably start smelling like him since you must ride him to Bend. Now let's give it a practice run. Get out your wand and jump on board."

Mimi took her wand out of her backpack. The wand's color had changed from white to a pale sky blue that glittered in the sunlight. While Mimi had her pack opened, Rosella stuffed Chatty into the bag. Mimi heard a squeaky, "Here we go. Ow not so hard"

Rosella snapped the top of the bag closed. "Too much of a good thing," She said to Mimi. "Up with you now."

Mimi concentrated hard and moved her wand up while flapping her wings. Much to her surprise, she landed with a plop on Joseph's head. He stood up and started flinging his head around. Mimi was able to grab the scarf to hang on.

"Settle down Joseph," Rosella said stroking his head. "That's just that little blue fairy you snorted at."

She looked at Mimi and told her to scoot back behind the bow. "You want to be on his neck and use your wand like a crop on the horse. A tap on the back and Joseph should go forward. A tap on either side and he should turn."

Rosella turned to Ravenia and said, "You know what to do. Go fly somewhere and call. Mimi and Joseph will find you." Ravenia flew away, disappearing into the trees. In a few minutes, Mimi heard the distinctive "caaww." Rosella looked at her and said, "Go find Ravina and then come back."

Mimi tapped Joseph with her wand. It glowed slightly radiating some heat. Joseph jumped forward almost knocking Mimi off. Rosella scolded her to slow down and turn Joseph left. Mimi pulled on the scarf and shouted "Whoa!" When Joseph was walking, Mimi tapped him ever so slightly on the right shoulder. He turned left. They heard the caaaw again but this time they were much closer.

Chatty crawled out of the backpack and inched up to Joseph's head before Mimi could grab her. "Oh, this is so much fun. I'm riding the bow and watching for danger. I bet you didn't expect to see me here." Joseph kept raising his head to see what was talking to him. But, of course, the tiny hedgehog was outside his vision. Mimi was so engaged in staying on and directing Joseph that Chatty's banter was like background music. All at once there was a "caaw" directly overhead. Despite the odds, the strange traveling companions found Ravenia.

Mimi called up, "Thank you Ravenia." The bird tipped her head slightly. She took off back to the gypsy wagon. Mimi managed to turn Joseph around and head back to the wagon where Rosella was waiting.

"We'll all sleep here. We'll leave in the morning." Rosella said. "Are you leaving too?" Mimi asked.

"Oh yes, I'm going to go look for your sister, Maribel. Looks to me like she could use my help."

CHAPTER 10: ENCOUNTER WITH THE GOBLINS

Mimi and her friends had been traveling for three days when they entered a high-walled pass. The days had been clear with light well into the evening. Mimi was surprised to find blue ink night skies filled with pinpoints of light and a large moon. She had spent so much time in the Cyan Castle and the surrounding thick aspen grove that she really hadn't seen the beauty of the night sky or engaged in star watching. Just last night she'd seen a shooting star.

Joseph had proved amazingly adept at finding food. He rooted out berries and mushrooms with his long snout. Mimi and Chatty ate anything he did. Ravenia was on her own up in the sky. But her regular CA-A-WS provided a clear guide for them.

The weather had gotten cooler as they had climbed up into the mountains. Mimi was starting to get her bird language skills back. She heard lots of birds gossiping about her little tribe as they travelled along. "Where are they going? Look at that strange group. Is that big animal dangerous? Is that a fairy? What is that little thing making all the chirping sounds?"

Mimi chose not to respond because she wasn't sure she would be understood. She was still very timid about using her skills. She didn't want to delay the group. She didn't know what dangers might lay ahead.

There had been rain one evening. Not the soaking kind. The little, small droplets that make one feel cleaner. Mimi had tipped her face up to the sky and let the water pour down on her. The light sprinkle had helped clean her off. She kept a little travel towel in her backpack, so she was able to towel herself dry.

Fortunately, the rain cleaned Joseph too, or as Rosella had said Mimi was getting used to Joseph's odor. After the rain, Mimi didn't notice his smell as much.

They traveled near small streams. They had water when they needed it. Mimi noticed the looks of creatures along the streams, frogs, toads, and snakes. She stayed away from all of them. The skies were full of flies, bees, wasps, dragonflies, yellow and blue butterflies. There were lots of wildflowers blooming in the grass, red, yellow, and white.

Mimi had to keep reminding herself that Ravenia knew the way.

She needed to be brave, "I come from a long line of leaders. I can travel alone." She would say to herself.

One morning, Mimi felt an odd shiver go down her spine. Joseph was just starting down the path. Chatty was talking more if that was possible, "I feel something. Do you feel it? Listen there is something in the brush. Did you hear rustling?"

Unfortunately, Mimi did hear the rustling. She was about to stop Joseph to investigate when she heard a snap and whiz. Joseph let out a terrible scream of pain like a baby dying. He took off like a rocket. Mimi caught a glimpse of pewter-colored reptilian skin disappearing into the bushes. She was hanging onto Joseph for dear life, pulling on Joseph's scarf, shouting "STOP!"

Chatty's eyes had gotten huge. She was pointing backward squealing, "Smoke beast, shooting rocks, drooling, blood."

Mimi thought to herself, "Oh no, we've encountered one of the dreaded smoke goblins." Mimi had never seen one but had read about them in books. Humans and fairies are both supposed to avoid them. They are hard to spot because their slate color helps them blend in with dirt and brush. They look like rocks lying about. They frequently wear red hats dyed in human or animal blood. Any goblin with a red hat is considered extremely dangerous and should be avoided. "Chatty, did you see any red?" Mimi asked.

"The smoke beast wears a red cap, blood dripping down its face. Red drool. Terrible! Terrible!" Chatty squealed as Joseph continued to gallop down the rocky trail. Ravenia was nowhere to be found.

"Thanks, Chatty. Quiet." Mimi shushed. "Joseph, you have to stop. We have to regroup with Ravenia. We can't walk into a troupe of red-hat goblins. They're killers."

At that moment, Joseph fell into a large hole that had been disguised by branches laid crisscrossed over the pit. "O-off," he grunted as he landed on his belly knocking out all his air. Mimi smelled Joseph's terrible musk order as if the hard landing had knocked all the gas out of him. She gagged and then puked on the smell. She was hanging tight to the purple scarf with one hand dangling down his neck. She was like an ornament on a Christmas tree wings and all. "Just as useless," she thought.

Chatty Cathy had tumbled off Joseph's head and was pinned under his front left hoof. She must have landed between one of his four toes or possibly in the conclave between hoof and leg.

"Are you ok?" Mimi asked Joseph. She got no response. She heard Chatty squeaking, "I'm stuck in a cave with no light. Everyone has left me. Come back! Come back."

"Quiet," Mimi said. "You're under Joseph's hoof. Are you hurt?"

"Hurt? Can't see. No pain. Don't know."

"I think you're fine. I have to get Joseph off of you. The goblins must have dug this hole to trap humans and other large animals. They're carnivores."

"What's that? Do they put us in cans? Maybe I'm too small."

"It means if they catch us, they'll eat us. I'm sure they will think you're a tasty little tidbit. A pre-dinner appetizer." Mimi heard sobbing coming from under the hoof. Ravenia came swooping down into the pit and pulled on Mimi's backpack with her large black beak.

"What are you trying to tell me?" Mimi asked. Ravenia pulled harder, then let go, flew out of the pit, and circled around, dove back in. This time she pulled so hard on Mimi that she let go of the scarf. Ravenia dropped Mimi by her wand which had fallen on the ground near Joseph. Mimi picked up the wand. She noticed a slight blueish glimmer. Ravenia circled so frantically that she lost a couple of black feathers that floated down to the ground. Mimi closed her eyes and focused on her wand and her wings. She willed herself to lift. Her wings started slowly moving. She rose out of the pit with her wand pointed straight up the tip barely glowing.

Once over the lip of the hole, her wand tipped straight left. But Mimi didn't follow where it was pointing because she was looking down the road to the right. A group of noisy goblins were assembling. They were coming out of a cave to join the one waving a slingshot. He must be telling them about the captured beast in the hole. There was a great deal of laughing and slapping each other on the back. All of them wore red hats. Some carried big sticks. A few had swords. This was not a crowd that Mimi wanted to fight.

Then she looked where her wand was pointing. There was a

large expanse of cobalt-blue water. "Crater Lake," Mimi thought. "Rosella told me I could get my wand recharged at Wizard Island. My wand is already getting some power just by pointing at the lake."

Chatty stopped crying and started shouting in a little high-pitched voice, "Scared. Don't know what to do. Trapped. Joseph dead. Crushed."

Mimi soothed Chatty, "I have an idea. My wings are working. We are very close to Crater Lake. I'm going to fly to the lake and try to get to Wizard Island. If I can recharge my wand, I can get you out and deal with the goblins."

Ravenia was circling high cawing. She headed towards the lake and then looped back over the pit. "Ravenia, I get it. I'm coming,"

Mimi shouted. "I'm going to try to make it to Wizard Island and get my powers back. Be back soon."

As she turned for the lake, Mimi could hear Chatty, "Don't go! Don't leave."

She heard Joseph grunt.

"At least he's alive," she thought. Then she headed straight for the crystal blue waters. She'd started off strong and her wand had enough charge to help pull her towards the lake. Her baby wings kept her in the air but didn't provide much thrust. As she flew, she could feel her wings tiring. As her wings got weaker, the pull of the wand grew stronger. That kept her going forward. She needed to find a way other than her wings to get to Wizard Island. Rosella had been right about her being a burden for Maribel. She was a burden even to herself. When her friends needed her most, she wasn't strong enough to help them. She had to recharge her wand and get back in time to fend off the goblins. Otherwise, Joseph would be Goblin Stew and Chatty Cathy the finger food.

CHAPTER 11: WIZARD ISLAND

Mimi stood in a tree near the lake, her hand shading her eyes from the intense sun. Before the Goblin incident, she awoke to a dazzling sunrise. The eastern skyline majestically shifted from dark to orange to burgundy to pink and finally a pale blue. But circumstances changed quickly. The glorious morning transformed in the blink of an eye into a horrible event.

Now she was focused on saving her friends. She surveyed a way to reach the island. One that didn't involve flying or swimming. She saw a dock and several large open boats parked and a sign; Shuttle to Wizard Island Every Hour Starting at 10.

"Shouldn't be long, before a boat goes," she thought. "I'll wait here and catch a ride on the boat."

Soon people started showing up and purchasing tickets at a little booth by the dock. Mimi floated down to the boat disguised as a butterfly. She saw a number of people point and say, "Look at the gorgeous blue butterfly." One mom grabbed her son and pointed at Mimi and said, "Look, Brian, you hardly ever see a blue butterfly."

Mimi was glad to hear the comments because it meant her colors were returning and her shape-shifting skill was also working. Obviously, it would have created a huge commotion if people were pointing and shouting, "Look at the wounded sooty fairy."

She found herself in a place that looked safe from human swats or finger touching. She sat at the front of the boat on the windshield. The engines began grinding. The captain gave the safety rules. He told the passengers how to find the life jackets. The boat pushed off.

Riding in front Mimi could see the big gray rock island sticking out of the bright blue lake. The lake didn't have the refreshing aroma of the ocean. There was a rotten fishy smell when a bloated dead salmon bashed against the boat. A high wind whipped the water into a frothy foam. The boat bounced up and down. Mimi would have preferred to shift back to fairy form to hang on. But she had already made herself visible. Drawing attention as a blue butterfly had created some danger so she stayed in butterfly form.

Swoosh, water drenched her and knocked her off her perch. Fortunately, she was flying well enough to flitter around for a short time and land on the lower part of the bow that was more protected. But the up-and-down splashing continued. There was the verbal monologue of the captain telling the history of the island. Mimi paid no attention. She had friends in danger. She needed her powers restored to help them. The purported powers of the island were her only hope of getting back to her former self and then helping her friends escape the goblin hole. Time was short.

The boat was finally within a few feet of the island dock. Mimi took flight and landed on the rocky gray shore. She could immediately feel the magic pull of the island. There were sounds all around her, whispers and o-o-os in low and high tones, shushing like Druids at Stonehenge. She wasn't exactly sure how to recharge her wand. She assumed she should look for a purple stone like Hannah had at the burl. She heard faint chimes erratically in the distance. She started flying towards the melodious sounds. She was heading up the island's rocky surface towards the top.

As she got closer to the peak, the whispers and low humming became louder. The chimes were more frequent. Mimi was hoping the top wasn't much further. She had rested a little on the boat ride. Holding her butterfly shape had taken all her energy.

Clinging to the boat as a butterfly had been difficult. She had depleted what little strength she had regained in her flight to the lake. She didn't have the reserves to fly much higher in search of the power source.

But she also couldn't give up. Her little team of two, Joseph and Chatty Cathy depended on her. She was the leader of her own fairy clan. She would think of her sister, Maribel. She would push longer and try harder. She knew that Maribel would do anything to save the fairies she loved. Mimi could do that too. She knew she could.

She was near the top. She almost flew into a group of humans traversing the trail from the dock. Several kids were running around chasing anything that moved including grasshoppers and chipmunks. Another kid was throwing rocks towards the lake. Mimi transformed into a rock. "I hope no one likes me and picks me up," she thought. With that in mind, she made herself extremely innocuous in a slate gray color with pointed sides. She didn't want to be picked up as a promising lake skipping stone. The humans marching by seemed oblivious to the increasing noise coming from the summit. "One must have special powers to hear the voices and tones," she thought. The noise was getting so loud that her ears hurt. Being a rock allowed her a small rest. She covered her ears to keep out the discordant sounds.

Once the humans had passed, Mimi unfurled herself. She took stock of her surroundings. There was a large dead tree with multiple long large broken branches. The tree had two large holes near the top slanting in different directions giving the appearance of a giant haunting scarecrow. "The horrible sound is definitely coming from the tree," Mimi thought. She felt a tingly feeling in the pit of her stomach. She was frightened. She knew she had to keep going forward. She was within five feet of the tree. A tremendous force surprised her and yanked hard on her wand. The indiscriminate noise she heard previously turned into ominous whispers hissing, "Give it here, give it here!"

"NO!" Mimi shouted at empty air. "I will not give up my magic wand." She pulled the wand close to her body. She could feel it starting to get warmer and when she peaked beneath her hand the blue color was returning to the base. "This is the source of the power," she thought. "Now all I have to do is find the source." Sweat was dripping down her brow from the effort to hold onto the wand. The wand was quivering in her hand.

Just as suddenly as the pull had started it stopped. There was an eerie still, silence all around her. Pink goose bumps popped out on her arms and little chills ran down her spine. Something alive was near her but she couldn't see or hear it. She transformed into a butterfly and waited patiently on a bush. Within a few minutes, the twigs lying on the ground picked themselves up and started walking around. The little twig dancers twirled around and skipped to a beat only they could hear. They had tiny stick hands and waved back and forth in the breeze. The dancing twigs had clearly fallen off the big tree but they definitely were not dead. Mimi thought, "The tree is probably not dead. These are its offspring."

Mimi slowly floated over them towards one of the holes in the big tree. The smallest twig stopped moving and pointed at Mimi. The other twigs stopped and looked too. She heard a voice say,

"Only a butterfly." Then the twigs went back to dancing until Mimi heard human voices on the path. The twigs dropped as a group and disassembled. By now she had reached the first hole. Mimi was used to objects looking like trees and being something else. After all, Mimi was born in Cyan Castle. Her birthplace looked like a giant fig tree to most people. The tree served as a state-of-the-art house for members of the Sapphire Clan. When she stared into the tree, she was greeted by the musty smell of decaying wood. Maybe she was wrong. Maybe this wasn't the centerpiece of power on Wizard Island. As she peered in further, she saw lights in the base of the tree, and she heard voices and laughter. "Ah, she thought, this tree is like my home. Someone lives in it. Whoever lived in this tree lived in the roots and burrows below the ground, not in the upper region.

She flew into the tree to see better. She was yanked by a tremendous power downward towards the noise. She quickly transformed back into a fairy so her delicate butterfly wings wouldn't be torn apart. Her wand was pulling her forward and getting brighter and warmer as she went. She wasn't sure what she would find but she knew she was headed towards the source of the magical powers on the island. She hit the bottom of the tree with a hard plop. Her long blue hair had flipped over her face and she couldn't see anything. When she flipped it back, she was staring a someone's feet. The someone was wearing gold boots with curled toes. When Mimi looked up, she was staring at a very tall, old man with a long white beard. He was dressed in a purple robe decorated with gold stars and golden braid. Mimi could feel this man's mystical power. She was in the presence of the Wizard for whom the island was named.

"Who are you child?" asked the Wizard in a deep melodious voice.

"I'm Mimi La Fay from the Sapphire Fairy Clan," answered Mimi in as strong a voice as she could. She was terrified. Her voice sounded a little high and squeaky. "I had to flee Cyan Castle because of fire. Then I was hurt and lost my clan."

"I'm sure there is quite a long story behind those few

sentences. But I can feel time is of the essence. Why have you come to me?" the Wizard asked.

"Rosella, the gypsy, told me to seek out Wizard Island to regain my power. I can tell by the increasing color and heat of my wand that there is the energy to recharge somewhere near."

"Ah, so you want a magic recharging gem," said the Wizard. "You have come to the right place."

Mimi grabbed his feet and hugged his ankles. "I'm so glad you can help me. My friends have been captured by red-hat goblins. I fear for their lives."

"You are wise to be afraid of the goblin tribe that lives on the banks of the lake. They are a mean and nasty group. They are the most bloodthirsty goblins I have ever met." He pointed to a corner where a large purple, multifaceted stone was glowing. "The magic amethyst is over there. If you place your wand against the stone and allow it to warm up, the wand will once again have magic powers. But you must hang on tight. I'm sure you've already felt the pull of the stone."

"Yes, that's what brought me to the tree. I was pulled down to you."

"The pull is only available to those magical creatures who have pure hearts. That is why I never fear the many different species of visitors I get. Only those who deserve to control magical powers are led here by the stone. Once the wand's powers are returned, you may find it hard to control at first. The wand will be like a young stallion released from a barn on a blustery day. Wands have a tendency to run wild. You wouldn't want to lose it."

"No, I have to keep it. I have to get back to my friends."

"The gem is waiting," said the Wizard pointing towards the stone. "Good luck! You are dealing with a bunch of brutes. You don't have time to dally around thanking me. Come again when you have time to visit."

Mimi ran over to the gemstone. She placed her wand on the rock. She did as the Wizard had instructed and held on with both hands. The wand started warming up very quickly. The color changed from chalky white blue to bright blue where her hands were. The color and warmth started moving up the wand.

"Come on, come on! Hurry, I need to get going." Mimi thought. Mimi's hands were extremely hot now. She wasn't sure she could hold on much longer. The pull of the wand was making her arms move up the stone until her arms were over her head.

Woosh. The wand took off. Shooting stars were coming out of the top of it. Mimi was being flipped all around the tunnel and then yanked up the inside of the tree and out into the open air. She could feel herself smiling. She was flying. Her wand was fully armed.

She snapped her wings. She heard a crack, crack. Air whooshed backward. She shot forward. Her wings felt different, heavier. She looked behind her. A miracle had happened in the tree root, her permanent wings had appeared. They were huge. SNAP! SNAP! They were powerful. She was shooting across the sky with each flap of the big wings. They were glorious shades of blue. Ombre design a pale blue on top shading into darker and darker blues with navy on the bottom. Mimi felt wonderful. No wonder her friends used to practice. She didn't have time now. After she took out those pesky goblins, she was taking these big boys for a ride.

Now if she just had her flight suit. "Bang!" She looked down, her legs and arms were covered in skintight silver. Her powers had become extremely potent at the purple stone. Her every wish was now a command. She looked like Maribel, a great warrior, only smaller.

"Those goblins are in trouble now," Mimi thought.

CHAPTER 12: BATTLE WITH THE GOBLINS

Mimi zipped off Wizard Island. She headed across Crater Lake. She didn't hesitate as she steered up the hill towards the Goblin pit. Her wings were working perfectly. Her wand was still shooting sparks of blue, like a sparkler on the 4th of July. Her long blue hair streamed behind her, a banner saluting her newfound strength.

"What a fabulous feeling to have the air rushing through my hair," she thought as she was propelled forward. "Rosella was right to send me to Wizard Island. With powers, I can battle for the first time. I can save my friends."

Mimi's enthusiasm was slightly diminished as she burst over the hill and descended to the lake. She could see goblins marching in pairs from their cave down to the pit. The first three sets of pairs were carrying heavy pots with steam rising from them. "O-oo, something very hot is in those pots," she thought. She transformed into a butterfly so she could get closer without the goblin's knowledge.

She fluttered over them. One of them swung a stick at her and almost landed a blow. "I have to be more careful," she thought. "These guys are just nasty to lash out at a harmless butterfly."

She could see that they were carrying boiling oil in the pots. The goblin in the lead said to his partner, "This hot oil should fix the fanged pig, Nail Head"

"Yes, you are very clever, Pounder," said Nail Head. "We kill the nasty beast with the oil. The oil cooks him and floats him to the top of the pit," Pounder's friend made a wicked laugh. "Yes, very clever indeed. I wasn't sure how we were going to get such a large, fanged beast out of the pit. I didn't know how to lift him on a stew pole. But you have figured out how to do it all at once. All of us, appreciate the work you have saved us with your thinking cap on."

"Yes, that is why I'm the leader. I'm more intelligent and stronger than the rest of you," bragged Pounder. He held his head up in the sun and preened. "Messy work getting down in the pit with a fanged beast. I haven't seen a pig like this before. Maybe he is a magic beast. I wonder what he will taste like? He is so big! He will provide many days of feasting."

"The goblinettes are very excited," said Nail Head. "My wife is putting on her best pots. When she bumps and grinds she will clang merrily."

"It is unfortunate that I lost my temper last week and threw my hatchet at my wife. She would have enjoyed the celebration today. But I have noticed some new young goblinettes. One with a new red hat is quite saucy and forward. I believe her name is Big Chin.

If it is not, it should be," Pounder laughed horribly at his own joke. "She has a huge, pointed chin with a large hairy mole in the middle that I find delightful. She has been flirting with me. I shall ask her to bump and clang this evening," mused Pounder.

As they were talking, they were continuing their slow walk down the trail from their cave to the pit. They were walking very carefully over the rocky terrain. Mimi assumed they didn't want to slop hot oil on themselves. If they spilled, they would lose so much of the oil on the walk that there wouldn't be enough to float poor Joseph to the top of the pit. She had to admit that Pounder's plan was a good one. She hadn't been sure how she was going to get Joseph out of the pit but the oil had given her an idea.

Pounder broke into singing, "Trouble, trouble, hot oil bubble.

Give us food and grow our stubble." Both Pounder and Nail Head set their pot down and started evil giggling. They linked arms and swung each other around in a circle. The others set their pots down to watch, laugh, and applaud.

Nail Head continued with a new verse, "Goblin, goblin, sure to scare. Give us food 'cause we don't wear underwear." A loud cheer went up from all the assembled men.

"We fight with hammers and axes, making blood galore," continued Pounder. "After we win, we seek out more gore." There was more cheering.

Mimi was wildly upset by their song. She was having trouble holding her butterfly shape. They had made her so angry she was turning a purplish pink.

"Time's a wasting, boys," shouted Pounder up the hillside. "Let's pick up those pots and go boil us a pig for dinner."

Mimi could hear high-pitched squealing and grunting coming out of the pit as the Goblin troops marched closer. She left the goblins behind to check on her friends. Changing back to a fairy, she swooped down to the edge of the pit.

Joseph was snorting, squealing, and running in circles. His hooves were making deep grooves in the bottom of the pit, kicking up dust. He was butting his tusks against the walls trying to escape. If he had enough time, he might be powerful enough to knock down enough dirt to make a ramp out. But with the goblins coming, the end was near.

Chatty Cathy was sitting in a corner behind a rock clump weeping. "We're doomed. Fairy left us. No one cares. I'm going to be eaten."

Mimi got down on her hands and knees, leaned over the pit, and shouted, "Quiet!" Both Joseph and Chatty stopped what they were doing and looked up at her in surprise. "Now I have my magic powers. The goblins' strength far outweighs my magic. We're going to have to depend on each other to get out of this. Do you both know how to swim?"

"I good swimmer, swim til I exhausted," said Chatty.

Joseph shook his head up and down and grunted which Mimi took as a yes.

"Ok, the Goblins are bringing hot oil. I'm going to change the oil to water. You must swim with all your might to get out of the pit. While you're swimming, I'm going to put a spell on the goblins. I can't keep them at bay forever. Joseph, you're going to knock them out of the way using your tusks and fangs. I will put Chatty on your back and then we will run for it. We are much faster than they are. They tend to be heavy-footed louts. They dress in old pots and pans and metal objects. Running must be awkward."

Mimi flew up in the air from the pit. The first row of goblins was a few feet away. She was thrilled when Nail Head called behind him, "Hurray up! We're going to drench this guy with oil all at once." Her spell would be easier to cast if all the pots were dumped together.

The next set of carriers was moving into position. They were setting their hot pot on the very edge of the pit right next to the first pot. Nail Head directed, "Move over there so we can get the third pot down here." Chatty and Joseph had moved to the far side of the pit from the pots. Chatty's eyes were popping out of her head staring at the oil.

"Me scared! Me scared!" she screamed. Mimi was worried Chatty might pass out from fright and not be able to swim. But

Mimi had to wait until the very last minute. She had her wand up in the air. She was hovering just high enough up that she hoped the goblins wouldn't see her and change tactics at the last moment.

The final pot was being moved into place. Nail Head was giving directions, but Mimi was focused on the pots. She must send the spell at just the right moment. Nail Head lined three goblins up behind each sizzling pot. "Now on the count of three," he thundered to the assembled group. "Dinner is a'coming. One, two, three, tip"

Mimi's wand went up on one. She started the incantation on two. "Water, water cool clear water. Boiling oil dissipates. Bring us water to swim and escape." On three, a blinding blue light burst from her wand. Mimi streamed the light across the three pots. The goblins helping with the pots jumped back, and others cowered.

Deep voices shouted, "Owe, hot, What's happening?" There was general confusion around the pit.

The clear water poured into the pit. Mimi was thrilled to see both Joseph and Chatty were able to swim. Their legs were paddling as the water rolled in. They went under a couple of times because of the turbulence but popped right back up.

Nail Head was looking to the sky. "There's a magical creature with us. Where is it?"

Before he could spot her, Mimi rolled out another spell, "Tutus, cantaloupe, banana, and cherry, clothe the goblins, make them merry. Have them dance like little girls, twirling and whirling until they are dizzy." Mimi's wand came down with a zing, blue star mist covering all the goblins. When the shiny fog dissipated, the goblins were dressed in brightly colored ballet costumes and dancing and prancing all over the hillside.

The water had filled the pit and was sloshing over. Joseph was swimming to the side. He was having trouble getting out of the pit with his great weight. Mimi lifted her wand, "Make some steps and make them quick." A small set of steps appeared on the steep edge of the pit. Joseph was able to get his footing and march out. Once out he shook all over. Water flew everywhere. Chatty had managed to pull herself out and was lying flat on her back with the sun shining on her belly. She was panting. Her little chest was moving up and down quickly. She was resting.

"Me alive. Me swim. Swim wildly," her weak, high voice said.

Mimi dove down to Joseph's eye level and said, "I'm going to ride you into battle. We are going to take out the leader and his lieutenant. They are dancing over there." She pointed at Nail Head, wearing a garish orange tutu. He was twirling at surprisingly high speed on his lumpish feet. He was wearing yellow pointe shoes with blue straps up his legs. Pounder was holding an excellent fourth position with his feet crossed and his arms forward as if embracing a large barrel. He was doing deep knee bends and then standing on his toes and spinning around. He was dressed in a plum organza skirt and parakeet slippers. Mimi was rather proud of her spell. All the goblins were busy and enthralled with their dancing. The problem was she had no idea how long it would last.

She landed on Joseph's ruff and directed him at Nail Head, "Get him," she shouted and pointed her wand at him. Joseph pawed the ground with one hoof and then the other. He made a mighty snort. He took off at full speed with his head down. He butted Nail Head directly in the belly. Nail Head was sent flying over the edge of the cliff. "Good Boy," said Mimi patting Joseph on the head. "Now the purple dancer."

Joseph whirled around on two legs like a stallion. He thundered towards Pounder. He hooked Pounder's tutu on his tusk and spun him around over his head, stomped on him with his foot, and then rolled him off the cliff. "That ought to hold them for a while, " Mimi said, patting Joseph. "Let's go get Chatty and get out of here."

Chatty was sitting up when they walked up to her. "Feelin' better. All dried out. Water out of lungs."

Mimi flew off Joseph's back and used her wand to lift Chatty up on his neck. Chatty kept talking but Mimi flew high enough up so she couldn't hear. She did hear Ravenia's call. She flew towards the sound. Ravenia had been watching the battle from a nearby tree. When Mimi flew up to her, she would have sworn the Raven winked at her.

Mimi said, "We're going to move double time. We don't know how long the goblins will be dancing. But since Joseph knocked their leaders out, I think they will take some time to organize. Bend or bust! Show us the way."

Ravenia flew off, and Mimi flew lower and behind. Joseph set off on the next leg of the journey at a speedy trot. Chatty was hanging on the purple bow on his neck bouncing up and down talking.

CHAPTER 13: WELCOME BY A GNOME

The little troop was exhausted as they came around the turn leading to Bend. They had outrun some straggling goblins who had been outside Mimi's spell range miles back. Joseph had trotted quickly. Ravenia's calls continued to lead the way. Mimi was pleased when she started seeing signs announcing Bend.

Mimi was dozing on Joseph's back when she was awakened by a 2-foot-tall gnome standing in the road waving his hands to stop. He wore a red pointed hat with a curve on the tip, a white beard, and a blue coat. She realized he was shouting something at them. She focused her attention on hearing.

"I'm Roam the gnome. You look like weary travelers. I run a bed and breakfast for magical creatures. I am happy to offer you a bed and refreshment."

Mimi stared at him wearily.

"You're very near Bend," he continued. "I'm inviting you and the little one (pointing at Chatty) into my modest digs for the night.

Your great beast and blackbird are on their own. I don't have room for either in my digs." The gnome started laughing until tears ran down his face. Mimi just stared at him. He looked up, wiped the tears away, and said, "Oh, you don't get the joke. I live underground in an old remodeled rabbit warren. The rabbits dug out a system of burrows underground. Believe me, it provides great lodging, protected from the elements and big critters."

Mimi responded "I've been thinking I should send Joseph and Ravenia home. Joseph is far from his southwest homeland. I don't think he likes cold at all. Ravenia belongs to a gypsy, Rosella."

"How you deal with your menagerie is up to you," harrumphed Roam. "I think they are not cultured enough to be in the magical city of Bend. You will find Bend is full of all kinds of whimsical beasts and people. We have fairies, elves, wizards, brownies, good witches. We have folks who practice the dark arts and sorcery. We have distasteful creatures like goblins and dwarfs. You need to take care. The two are not always easy to distinguish."

Mimi interrupted him, "Believe me, we know about evil goblins. We barely escaped a tribe of red-hatted smoke goblins today."

Roam continued on as if she'd said nothing, "We have many shapeshifters so you may meet someone who appears to be human and turns out to be a snake," Roam finished making "snake" sound like a deep hiss.

"I've never been around humans," Mimi explained. "The Cyan Castle was totally protected by a huge aspen forest. The only group I've lived with besides the Sapphire Clan was the Treewicks. They are a lovely elf family. They let me share their home when I was hurt. I am a member of the Sapphire Clan."

"Yes, yes," Roam interrupted impatiently as if Mimi should know he would be informed of her background. "Professor Magnus saw you coming in his gazing ball. That's why I'm standing out here. Do you think I just stand around all day waiting for creatures to pass by? You are a silly fairy. But then many fairies are silly. They have such wee brains" Mimi didn't have time to be offended. Roam just kept talking. "I'm a very busy gnome. I welcome travelers. I do TV commercials. I help Professor Magnus with his research. Professor Magnus is a fairyologist. He's an expert on fairy lore."

"Just today, he saw you all suited up in sliver with giant blue wings."

Mimi interrupted, "Aren't they gorgeous!" She snapped them a couple of times. Sending air vibration around her.

" I was right. You are a silly creature," snapped Roam. "You just interrupted me with your useless flapping. Your wings look like many fairy wings. They are just big for your body. I'm no judge of their beauty."

"Sorry for interrupting." Mimi apologized. "I'm just thrilled to have permanent wings. Since you don't have wings, you can't know how exciting they are."

"Apology accepted. I think. Seemed a little weak to me. No need to point out I'm flat-footed. I travel rapidly anyway." Roam said, grumpily. "As I was saying, determining you were part of the Sapphire Clan didn't take much detective work. But he also saw a gorgeous fairy woman dressed like you. He thought you might be from the same clan or related... The ball clouded blood red and everything disappeared. The Professor was very interested. He didn't know there was a fairy battle underway in North America. He thought maybe the image was from Scotland."

"No, that's wrong. You saw Maribel, my sister. I saw that same vision with Rosella," exclaimed Mimi excitedly. "Rosella is a gypsy, and she has a magic gazing ball too. I wish you knew where Maribel is. I think whatever remains of the Sapphire Clan will be with Maribel. I really should join them."

"You can't be flying hither and there looking for them. Come in and get rested." Roam directed. "We'll get a plan together tomorrow with the help of the Professor. He's very smart and has all kinds of information about fairies and their history. You might learn something." Roam started walking away towards a hole in the ground. He turned back waved for Mimi to come and said,

"Oh, and release your beasts. They really don't fit in my inn. They should be getting back to their homes."

Mimi picked up Chatty from in front of her, patted Joseph on his ruff, and fluttered down to the ground. She placed Chatty carefully on the ground. Chatty immediately started mumbling, "Can't leave a person in peace, finally got used to the beast and he's goin'."

Mimi looked down to shush Chatty and saw a tear leak out of her eye. She understood Chatty's anguish. She was going to miss the big lumbering beast, who had found them food, served as their ride, and saved their lives. But she also understood Roam's point. Joseph didn't blend in well in city surroundings. He certainly wouldn't fit into a rabbit warren. She would be putting him at risk to keep him. People might be frightened of him or want to kill him for food. She didn't know the climate. If it was cold, he might freeze. It was best to send him to his southwest home.

"Joseph, Chatty and I have loved getting to know you. You are the finest stead I have ever ridden. You stay the course, hunt for food and you are brave in battle. If we were at Cyan Castle, I would have my sister knight you and invite you to stay. But we are still far from home. I'm not sure where we will go next. I release you from the charge Rosella gave you. You have delivered us safely. You may return home."

A tear rolled down her cheek as she said these words. She reminded herself she must remain brave for Joseph's sake. She called out to the sky, "Ravenia!" and then whistled. The black raven appeared from the trees and landed on the ground right in front of Mimi. She looked directly into Mimi's eyes with her alert onyx eyes.

"Ravenia, you've done well. You guided us to Bend. Now you

have a new job before you. Return to Rosella. You must guide Joseph to safety. Don't leave him until you know he can find his way home. Do you understand?"

Ravenia nodded her head and scratched the ground with her giant talons.

"I wish you well, my magnificent guide. Give my greetings to Rosella. My intuition tells me I will see both of you in the future."

Ravenia winked and took to the air. She swooped around Joseph and caa-wed. Joseph snapped to alert tracking the big bird with his ears, nose, and eyes. He started out at a strong trot. As they disappeared around the corner and into the big trees, both Mimi and Chatty openly cried.

Mimi patted Chatty's head, and said, "Two friends going home. We should wish them well and feel joy for them. But my heart hurts."

Chatty chirped through her sobs, "Me too, me too. Lonely"

"Come along," shouted Roam, "Enough blubbering out there to fill a swimming pool." He was now waving at them from the entrance to a hole.

Chatty walked cautiously into the dark entrance, "I'm scared, can't see anything." Roam gave Chatty a smack on the butt, "Get along little fella, time's a wasting."

Chatty jumped forward shrieking, "Ow!" followed by a highpitched squeal echoing farther and farther away. Chatty was clearly dropping from a high height landing who knows where. Finally, a little squeak and silence.

Mimi, thankful for her wings, chose to jump into the blackness with her wings fluttering. She used her wand like a flashlight. She was glad she did. She slowly descended more than 30 feet down a rocky cavern. There were handholds like a climbing wall not visible without her light and not scalable by a hedgehog. When Mimi touched down on the rocky bottom, Chatty was walking around. Her fur was puffed out all over from the wind velocity of the fall. Her eyes popped out from the experience. The fact that she could walk was a good sign. At least she hadn't broken anything, most of all her voice box. Chatty was chirping about, "Fall terrible, wind noise, hair pulled out, no landing pad."

As Chatty was rambling on, Roam dropped in. He landed casually in a crotched position and stood right up scolding "If you're going to explore the world properly you really need a magical way to get from one place to another. Your hedgehog is definitely not meant for exotic travel."

"Did I mention, I'm a celebrity? I've been on TV. I pop up on lots of people's vacations usually in their rooms and surprise them with awards." Mimi had never seen TV up close. She'd seen it in the windows of human campers just like she'd heard songs on the boom box. But she wasn't going to inform this grouchy little man of her ignorance.

" I can tell by your faces you aren't aware of my notoriety, so I won't offer you an autographed picture or gnome mug," Roam continued on without waiting for Mimi to answer. This seemed to rather a habit of his." Let's traverse down the hall to my quarters.

As I told you, I run a bed and breakfast. Dinner isn't my gig. The Professor asked me to provide you with dinner. I whipped up cricket with blackberry stew. It was what I had easily around."

A delicious aroma of hearty stew greeted the threesome as they walked down the tunnel. Mimi was contemplating what cricket stew might taste like. Roam seemed to read her mind because he turned and said, "I broke off their heads and limbs. Some folks don't like eyes swimming by in their stew and once in a while a leg can be like a chicken bone and get stuck in your craw. Most folks really enjoy the stew. The cricket skin gives it a nice crunch when you bite down, and the berries make it a little sweet. Has the texture of syrup and the taste of sweet and sour."

Chatty forgot about dropping down the entrance and started talking about the food, "Me hungry, yum, yum."

Roam turned to Mimi and said, "You've got to find a better traveling companion than a talking hedgehog. All that nonsense all the time would drive me crazy."

"Oh, Chatty's not so bad," Mimi defended her friend. "The journey was really long and scary. Chatty's chatter made it seem mundane. She doesn't expect you to listen or respond. She just likes to talk."

"If you ask me sounds like my senile grandmother," grumbled Roam.

Mimi was quickly learning that Roam was not very charitable. He was only hosting Chatty and her because of the Professor. Mimi was very thankful the Professor had seen them coming and Roam was waiting for them. They had reached Bend late. She had no idea how to establish new connections. She was tired, dirty, and hungry. Dinner, a bath, clean clothes, and a bed would be delightful after a number of nights sleeping on the ground.

The nights out on the ground had not been unpleasant. Growing up in a tree, Mimi had really not experienced the night sky. The first night lying on the ground looking up she thought of a silky cloth, dyed in a dark inky wash with a star dust pattern. The glowing golden sliver of the crescent moon was like a fabulous pin on an elegant sable scarf holding the sky up in the heavens. The travelers had been lucky that the weather had been dry and cool, except for the one cleansing sprinkle. They had slept on piles of leaves the colors of paprika, caramel, and ginger. The leaves were warm and surprisingly soft. When one of the threesome moved the leaves crackled. The soft rustle was calming rather than alarming. The sounds of the leaves crunching, Joseph's snores and Chatty's mewling reminded Mimi she was not alone. A thought she found very comforting.

When they reached the end of the tunnel Mimi found herself in a huge great room with a roaring fire. The stew pot hung on a spit across the flames merrily bubbling away. There was a large table with benches in the center of the room. The place was quite charming. Roam quickly dished up the stew and gave them water. They ate their stew in silence. Chatty had to be exhausted or terrified of Roam to be so quiet. When dinner was over, Mimi asked where her bedroom was. Roam looked at Chatty and pointed her towards a pallet on the floor by the fire. Chatty ran over to it and immediately lay down. Mimi saw no point in making a fuss if Chatty was happy with the accommodations.

Roam turned to Mimi, "Come with me. I think you'll be pleased." They walked down another dark tunnel lit by a few candle sconces with several doors. Roam stopped at a door painted pink with a red heart cut-out. He said, "Welcome to the princess room."

The door opened. Mimi was amazed to see a large room decorated entirely in different shades of pink. A circle covered with pink and white carnations was attached to the ceiling. Gauzy blush fabric floated down covering a large queen-sized bed, more than enough space for a fairy. The bed had a fluffy bubblegum-colored bedspread accented with flamingo pillows. A beautiful plush magenta blanket lay across the foot of the bed. The bed sat on a giant red raspberry heart-shaped rug. The floors were entirely covered with white oak planks. The walls behind the bed were painted hot pink and covered with climbing white roses. The other three walls were a softer shade, a pale rosy peach. A chandelier made of heart-shaped crystals hung in the center of the room. The tiny pieces of glass reflected hearts all around the room. There was a small white brick fireplace with a fire burning. A punch bowl was sitting in the corner filled with steaming pink bubbles, perfect for a fairy bath. The room had the faintest waft of sweet, fruity rosewood.

Roam bowed and put his hand forward as a sign that Mimi should enter. "I hope you are satisfied with your accommodations. Professor Magnus wants to meet you tomorrow."

Mimi turned to Roam and took his gnarled hand in her tiny blue smooth ones. "Roam, this is so much more than I could have hoped for. I so appreciate help from a complete stranger. Thank you so much."

Roam ducked his head hiding his emotions, he answered, "It is nothing. A beautiful fairy deserves comfortable accommodations." With that, he closed the door. Mimi was alone. She could hear him marching back down the hall to the great room. As he left, she realized she had not said, "Good Night." "Too late now," she thought. Tomorrow would come soon enough. Tonight, she was going to take advantage of the bath and luxurious room.

CHAPTER 14: PROFESSOR MAGNUS AND THE MAGIC BOOK

Mimi was seated on a small book eating a mini muffin off a pile of more books on top of a large desk in a crowded office. The sign on the door when she flew in read, "Professor Magnus, Folklore Specialist and Fairyologist."

Mimi had used her wand to create her royal apparel. She knew she had to be careful not to use her powers for frivolous activities. Having just recharged her wand, she understood how important it was to conserve fairy power so the energy would be available in an emergency.

But this was the first time Mimi had ever met a human, other than the gypsy, much less talked with one. She wanted to be on an equal footing, so she'd dressed up for the occasion. She burned her old clothes from the journey last night.

Today, she was dressed in the traditional garb of the Sapphire Clan. She had tried to copy Maribel's outfit when she was installed as clan leader. Mimi had on a long flowing blue skirt. She wore a blue-white tartan scarf over her white blouse. Her half medallion of the fig tree was proudly displayed on a gold chain around her neck. The sapphires were bright but not glowing as they did when combined with Maribel's half of the medallion.

When she had joined Professor Magnus for brunch she had been surprised by his appearance and demeanor. He had clearly not thought the occasion special. He was dressed in a rumpled suit, there was a coffee stain on his shirt and his tie was askew. He was heavy set and had a bald head with shoulder-length wispy white hair serving as a fringe around his scalp. Right now, his hair on the right side was sticking straight out where he'd just run his hand. He wore silver-wire framed reading glasses perched halfway down his nose. He had prickly hairs growing on his chin as if he had not shaved in several days. In fact, he looked like he'd slept on the couch in the corner where there was a mushed-up pillow and brown blanket thrown to the side.

He and Mimi exchanged names. He'd told her to call him, "Magnus." And then he'd thrown the muffin at her. Mimi grabbed it and thought, "Good grief, good thing I'm a good catch or the muffin would be smashed on the floor."

Mimi was helping herself to the muffin, cranberry, as the Professor directed the conversation. "You like muffins, do you?" he asked but didn't wait for an answer. "I'll note that in my research records. You behave very much like a small human."

Mimi thought to herself, "What does he think a fairy is? We are small humans except we can fly and do magic. We are actually more talented than humans, just small." She kept these thoughts to herself thinking Jaygo would tell her she was quite outspoken. Oh, how she missed her friends.

By way of introduction, Magnus said, "I study fairies. I record everything about them I can. I hope you don't mind if I record our conversation. I've established a fairy sanctuary here in Bend for fairies who have lost their homes or are hurt. I've met several blue fairies in the past. But of course, it's a pleasure to meet you. Do you mind if I turn on my phone to record our conversation?" Mimi nodded her head but didn't answer because she was chewing on a berry. She didn't want to talk with her mouth full.

After that introduction, they discussed how Mimi had become lost and arrived in Bend. Mimi didn't find this conversation very interesting because she had lived through it. Here and there, the Professor interjected questions but mainly he let Mimi describe her experiences. She'd just gotten to how she wanted to find her clan when she saw the gazing ball, sitting on the corner of the desk. As she was talking about Maribel, clouds started forming in the globe. She could see a silhouette of a female fairy emerging. She was sending out lightning strikes with her straight royal-blue wand. There were no other distinguishing features except the wand and long white hair. Mimi was sure it was Maribel. She pointed at the gazing ball, "Magnus, look an image is emerging I'm sure it's Maribel, my sister! I'm looking for her. Do you know where that image is coming from?"

When she asked about the image in the globe, the Professor jumped up from his desk, dropped his entire muffin on the floor, and dashed around the room pulling books from his bookshelves and flinging them to the floor after flipping through a few pages. Now he was standing in the middle of the office, his hand pressed to the top of his head and muttering in a loud voice, "Now where did I put that book? I know I had it here somewhere." He got down on his hands and knees and crawled along the floor looking carefully at the titles of the big leather books, lowest to the floor.

"Here it is," he said to himself. He pulled out a giant book entitled, *History of Fairies in Northern California*. He set the book down next to Mimi. When he opened it up, the pages were empty.

He lifted a pointer at his desk and commanded, "Tell me about the Sapphire Clan." Mimi's attention was now fully engaged.

The pages started flipping forward and backward. As they moved, writing and gorgeous pictures appeared. When the pages stopped moving, Professor Magus sat down, pushed his glasses up again on his nose, and stared carefully at the page. The book began talking and showing pictures.

"HISTORY OF THE FAIRIES OF NORTHERN CALIFORNIA," the book said in a deep voice. Mimi was surprised and looked all around to make sure the voice was coming from the book. But only the Professor and she were in the room. The deep bass voice kept talking.

"The Sapphire Clan, sometimes called the Blues, live in Cyan Castle. The Cyan Castle is a giant fig tree hidden in an Aspen grove in Northern California. The grove sprang from a single seedling. The single seedling was planted by leaders of the Sapphires from Scotland. The leaders planted the first seedlings together as a symbol of their commitment to live in peace." Mimi knew all this from her history classes. She was amazed the book could talk. She sat transfixed waiting to hear what the book said next.

The book continued telling her history. A tiny Aspen tree sprang out of the book and spread roots all over the page with other tiny aspens shooting up towards the professor. In the center of the aspens on the page was a giant fig tree. The Aspens roots started creeping off the page and wrapping around the pencil holder and into a dirty coffee mug. A tree promptly sprouted.

"Ok, ok," said Professor Magnus. "I know about Aspens and how they're the largest living thing on the planet. Pull your trees back in and keep reading."

Professor Magnus manually turned the page and trees and roots all slithered back into the pages. They made a hushed whispering sound as they departed as if they had more to say. All the air was being squeezed out of them.

The next page flipped open, and a disc spun out onto the professor's desk glowing gold in the dim office light and reflecting tiny light specks on the office walls. The medallion bounced back to the page. There was a gorgeous fig tree with a giant leaf canopy and long roots. The leaves were covered with sparkling blue fairy lights. The base of the tree was surrounded by jade. Professor Magnus reached down to pick up the jewelry. Before he could touch the exquisite ornament split and all the color drained from it. The glorious medal became a black-and-white drawing with a caption underneath.

The book began talking again. "When the leaders planted the Fig tree, they also had a single medallion made. The two leaders split the medallion in two and agreed to share their powers. Each leader always carries one-half of the medallion. When the medallion pieces are combined, the power is doubled. For generations. the leaders of the Sapphires kept their pieces separate and lived in peace."

Mimi interrupted the book. She was wildly excited, "Look, Professor, I have half the medallion on me just like the picture."

"I know," the Professor said. "I noticed it as soon as you flew in.

I've read all about it. But, of course, to get to see it is a rare honor. I got this book out because it talks about your clan."

"I'm going to skip a lot of this." The Professor cut Mimi short.

"Much of it is your family history and you probably know it. But I'm going to try to jump to the most important piece to see if the book knows where Maribel and your clan are. I would really like to meet your sister sometime. I have never met a clan leader. That would be a unique find and make me famous."

The professor turned back to the book, tapped it with the pointer, and said, "Tell me about the Maribel."

The pages flipped back and forth and stopped as a picture of Maribel appeared. She looked gorgeous with her royal blue skin, violet eyes, white hair, and iridescent wings. She held a straight blue wand and was in her warrior apparel.

"That's Maribel!" Mimi shouted excitedly. "You have a picture of Maribel."

The book began again. "Maribel LeFae is now 18. She is a direct descendant of the Scottish LaFae family. She is considered a great beauty among fairies."

Mimi giggled when the book pronounced "booty" instead of beauty.

The book was not deterred by Mimi's snickers. "The Sapphires have not fought for generations. Since her home was burned, she is becoming known as a great warrior. The book intoned as if it was giving a lecture. Mimi was so excited she could hardly sit still. This was the first she had heard of her sister since the Peregrine Falcon had dumped her in the redwood.

This time the professor interrupted. "Does this sound like your sister, Mimi?"

"Oh yes!" exclaimed Mimi. "She is gorgeous and extraordinarily strong. She's great with her wand skills."

The professor tapped the book, "Go on now."

"Maribel helped her clan escape the great Paradise Fire. They sheltered at the Sacramento River. Most of the clan was saved from the fire."

This time Mimi interrupted that book. "I am so happy. This is the first time I've heard how my clan and sister got through the fire. Can the book tell us where she is?"

Professor Magus tapped the book with his pointer again and said, "Where is Maribel now?"

The book flipped from front to back, the pages whipping air in

Professor's Magus face and making his white hair stand out. Then all the pages flipped back to the first page.

The book said, "Cyan Castle and the surrounding Aspens were recently destroyed by the fires. There is no record of where Maribel Lafae and the Sapphire Clan are. Reports indicate her younger sister, Mimi, was lost in the fire."

"Wrong!" Mimi shouted at the book. "I'm sitting right here very much alive. You're not as smart as you think Mr. History book."

"Calm down." Professor Magus said. "The book only reports what it's been told. I'll make arrangements for corrections. You are obviously very much alive."

Professor Magus slammed the book shut and said, "I know what my next research must be. I must find this Maribel!"

"Me too," said Mimi. "I can be a big help to you. See the gazing ball, I made her silhouette appear."

"So you did." The professor put his finger on his chin and tipped his head. "I must think about how we should approach this. You have no idea where she is?"

"No," but the gypsy Rosella was going to look for her in Southern California. She thought she had moved the clan away from the fires south to safety."

"Let me think for a minute." The Professor said. Then he just sat silently staring at the empty globe. Mimi was getting antsy. She wanted to get started on her quest to find Maribel and her clan.

Finally, the Professor said to her, "I think you will find Bend a fascinating city. We are an eclectic mix of magic and whimsical creatures and humans. We have witches and warlocks who have trained to practice magic for good. Of course, like anywhere we have humans who engage in the dark arts. We also have wizards and Gypsies. We have a special fairyland. I think you will be amazingly comfortable there." The Professor concluded.

"But I don't want to go to some weird fairy asylum," Mimi objected. "I'm not a refugee. I'm the sister of the leader of a great clan. I must find them. Rosella sent me here because she thought I would be a burden when I was injured. But I have recharged my powers. I'm flying with permanent wings. I have control of my wand. I would rather go look for the Maribel and the Sapphires than settle into a fairy village." Mimi complained.

"Tell me if I am right. You've never been outside your aspen grove until you were forced out by fire."

"Correct!"

"You've never interacted with people."

"Right"

"You want to travel somewhere, we're not sure where and find your clan?"

"Right."

"It seems to me that you will need some guidance. You are hoping to find your sister. But hope is not a strategy." Magnus cautioned.

Mimi was surprised by the Professor's words. She had been raised to think of humans as dangerous brutes hell-bent on destroying the natural world. People should be avoided at all costs. Here she was having a normal conversation with a human who seemed to want to help her.

"What do you suggest?" Mimi asked.

"First, I am an academic wizard. My focus is on learning. I only have occasional success with the gazing ball. We can give it a try but I can't guarantee results. I am not a gypsy so I can't give you guidance through the cards. I am trying to caution you that I can help you create a decision tree but you'll have to decide what you should do. I think you should look at your options and choose your own path. Does that make sense?"

Mimi felt a little disappointed. She had hoped the Professor could open a book, order up a map, and tell her how to find Maribel and her clan. Apparently, that was not going to happen.

"My first suggestion would be you leave the hedgehog with Roam. The hedgehog is not an easy creature to transport. Roam has been lonely. I can see by the way he was complaining about all the chatter. He is quite taken with the little critter."

Mimi was incredulous. She had gotten an earful from Roam this morning about how annoying Chatty's joyful, "Morning, Morning, food, food, hungry." had been. He had even said, "I don't see how you stand listening to her high-pitched voice before coffee." Mimi wanted to be polite so she responded, "My travels would be easier without Chatty Cathy. But I don't think Roam really likes her as a pet."

"Nonsense! Roam told me he'd be happy to take her when I asked." The Professor smiled encouragingly.

"If, you're sure."

"Oh yes, so that's one problem solved. See how simple things are when we take each part one at a time," smiled Professor. "Chatty has a new home. You don't have to worry about the safety of an animal that isn't magical. As far as I can tell, Chatty Cathy has no skills. I think it was a little sneaky of the gypsy to just hand you the hedgehog. I am amazed you made it on your own with a javelina and a tiny foreign pet. Someday, your travels will make a great story."

"Now we are to the true dilemma. Do you rest here in fairyland, regroup, and possibly make friends to undertake an expedition? Or do you set out on your own with no experience to find your clan?"

"When you say it like that, it doesn't sound very smart to just take off from here right now," Mimi said a little morosely. She had wanted to take flight immediately and seek out Maribel. Her mother had warned her when she was little that she was too impetuous.

"It seems we have another decision made," smiled Professor. "You should take a place in Fairyland. From there, you can try to get a message to either Rosella or your sister. If everyone is moving around, the messages will never get where they are supposed to go. Just think of it. Eagles, owls, and ravens flying here and there with carefully written notes. The fliers move endlessly around trying to find the notes' owners."

"I hadn't thought of it that way," Mimi said. "I could stay in Fairyland and send out messages until one is answered. Is that your suggestion?"

"It is one option. But you are the one who must choose. If you choose that option, I will get you settled in Fairyland. Why don't you go to your room, take your time, and decide? The choice is, stay or go. If you stay, you should write Maribel and Rosella. I will send my fastest two owls to hunt for them to deliver your messages.

When you hear back, you will know how to proceed."

****

Mimi sat at the little white writing desk in the heart princess room. She was holding a bright green parakeet feather in both hands. Her mind was like a tumbling blender, "Stay or go? Stay or go? But where would I go? Who would I travel with?" She scolded herself, "You sound like Chatty Cathy unable to make a decision."

She finally stood up and started writing, *"Dear Maribel, when you get this note, know I am safe in Fairyland, in Bend, Oregon. I await word from you. I can't wait to see you and join the Sapphires again. I have had many adventures since I saw you. I have learned that you were right about my old friends. They weren't really friends. I've discovered through my travels that a good friend helps and supports you when your family can't. I've made some very good friends while traveling. Your loving sister, Mimi."*

As she finished the note, she realized that home was where your heart is not a physical location. Her heart would always be with the Sapphire Clan. As she thought about how she loved her sister and her fellow clan members, the jewels on her medallion lit up very brightly for just an instant.

Made in the USA
Columbia, SC
10 March 2024